CORNERED
Louis King

Black Gat Books • Eureka California

CORNERED

Published by Black Gat Books
A division of Stark House Press
1315 H Street
Eureka, CA 95501, USA
griffinskye3@sbcglobal.net
www.starkhousepress.com

CORNERED

ISBN: 979-8-88601-138-8

Text design by Mark Shepard, shepgraphics.com
Cover design by Jeff Vorzimmer, ¡caliente!design, Austin, Texas
Proofreading by Bill Kelly

First Stark House Press/Black Gat Edition: April 2025

"*Cornered* is fast paced and action packed, but with a character driven plot, portraying two individuals confronted by both external and internal conflicts facing a series of continual crises, any one of which can destroy them either physically or emotionally."—Bill Kelly

Cornered...

"When I married her I thought it was the most wonderful miracle that ever happened to me. Me, a dumb cop with a girl like that loving me. She was the miracle ... and when she died I figured it was the end of the world. Well, I was wrong on both counts. Betsy was the miracle, and my world doesn't end while she is here to look after. Don't keep this kind of talk up, Vic, or we split. I mean it."

Grogan sat down again, exhausted. He didn't want to talk about it any more.

"You don't mean that, Steve. You speak of doing what Henderson wants. Do you think you could trust him? Say you sell out, go back, you get on the stand and lie. You refuse to identify Henderson. He goes free. Do you think he would let you alone after that? Let you live? What is going to happen to Betsy when Henderson finally gets you?"

There it was again. Vic was right. Henderson would never let him go while they both lived.

CHAPTER 1

The girl standing beside the piano moaned softly into the microphone. ". . . and one more for the road." The words were barely audible. They could not have been heard at all through the normal hubbub of the bar, but the noise was hushed for this girl. Not entirely quiet, there was nothing premeditated about it, but glasses were set down more softly, casual conversations were whispered or stopped altogether, and all attention was centered on the singer. Even the whirling clatter of slot machines was momentarily stilled.

Grogan left his beer untouched on the table before him and sat watching her from the dimness of the booth at the back of the room. He grinned a little to himself. She had something, all right. Not a singing voice, but in this league it got her by. Perhaps the husky, sexy timbre of it made up for the lack of volume or pure tonal quality. Maybe it was just her looks—the clinging black dress accented her slimness and the paleness of her face and shoulders. A startling paleness, in this country of blazing sun and mahogany tans.

The song ended to a spattering of applause. Grogan watched the girl move between the tables, toward him. He stood up, conscious of the stir of excitement which always touched him in her presence.

"Hello, Grogan. Still waiting around the stage door trying to seduce the poor working girl?"

Her speaking voice was very unlike her singing. It was matter-of-fact, unaccented. She seemed deliberately to comb out the sultry overtones which she poured into the microphone. Her present smile did not have the slow, languorous allure caught by the spotlight; it was quick, friendly, almost a grin.

"Sure. The beer will flow in rivers."

"Not for me, it won't." She slid into the booth. Grogan seated himself opposite her. "I told Johnny to bring us over a bottle of champagne."

"Okay."

She looked at him, suddenly serious. "It is okay, isn't it Grogan? I mean, you really are on-the-level rich? I could drink beer if I had to. I'm more the champagne type, but you'd be surprised how often I make do with beer."

Grogan laughed. "I'm on-the-level rich. So far as drinking goes, anyhow. I might have trouble matching yachts with some of the boys around here."

"That's all right. I'll sit in bars with you, Grogan, because I know how to look after myself in bars, but yachts are a little out of my line. I might not feel so safe on a yacht."

The blond bartender stood beside the table. "Here you are, Terry. Best in the house, like you said."

The bartender poured champagne for Terry. Grogan shook his head, waving away the stemmed glass the man started to put before him.

"Why won't you join me?" she asked. "You ruin the tone of the table."

"Nobody can see us, back here in the dark. I don't like the stuff."

Terry watched the bubbles rising in her glass. "Like it? What's that got to do with drinking champagne? It makes me feel I've hit the big time."

Grogan could never be sure whether her irony was

meant for herself or him. Drinking domestic champagne in the bar of a second-rate desert clip joint.... For all her surface toughness, she was out of place here.

He was content to sit across from her, admiring the smoky depths of her blue eyes, the way her tight dark curls, framed the pale oval face. She was young, in the early twenties, and Grogan knew that was ten years too young for him. Anyway, such things were behind him.

"Why so glum, Grogan?" she asked. "You're glaring at me."

"You ought to get out in the sun more."

Terry extended a hand across the table, letting the hooded lamplight fall on her slender white arm.

"And get that all brown?" she asked. "Lose my stock in trade? It isn't easy for a girl to look naked here, the way the amateurs run around the pool in the daytime. Even in evening dress, I can't go much farther than the cash customers and not have it fall off. I try to get that undressed look by being a different color. Effective, don't you think?"

Grogan grunted. It was effective, of course. He hadn't analyzed it that way, but his own attention had probably been drawn at first by the illusion of nudity.

"Don't talk like that," he said.

She patted his hand. "Be reasonable, Grogan. I'm a working girl, and I have to get by on what I have. It isn't my voice, we both know that. I tried radio once and fell flat on my face."

"What's in it for you?" he asked. "In the long run, I mean. Do you intend to stick with this racket?" They had never talked seriously like this before.

"I may not have to stick with it. I may catch myself

a big butter-and-egg man first. That's what I've always heard them called. Are you a butter-and-egg man, Grogan?"

Grogan knew she didn't mean it, but he was uncomfortable. Damn, the complications a man got himself into.

"I was kidding," she said quickly. "I know you aren't, of course. Butter-and-egg men don't have cauliflower ears."

Grogan's fingers touched the faint thickening of his left ear. "This isn't . . ."

"And don't tell me that isn't a cauliflower ear. My old man was a pug, and I know a tin ear when I see one. How did you make your money, Grogan? It wasn't in the ring, because I would have heard about you if you were that good. We used to talk nothing but fighters around our house."

She didn't expect an answer, of course. Grogan wondered what she would say if he gave her one. It wasn't the sort of crack you make to a girl in a bar. You can't just smile and say: "I married a rich woman. She left me all her money when she died."

Then he forgot the girl entirely as his attention was caught by the man who came in through the front door. Down the length of the long room, dimly lit though it was, Grogan recognized him the moment he stepped inside. There was no mistaking the swagger of those slight shoulders, or the cast of those lean, dark features. Dandy Jim DeCarlo. And Dandy Jim knew Grogan just as well as Grogan knew him.

Dandy Jim put his back against the bar and looked the room over, slowly and carefully. It might mean nothing; he was a careful man. He certainly couldn't penetrate the murkiness of the booth at the rear. But he had the entrance bottled up tight. Grogan felt a heightened twist of the fear which never really left him now.

"Steve, what is it? Have you seen a ghost?" Terry's voice was no longer bantering.

"More or less. Is there a back way out of this place?"

"Only through the dressing room...."

"That will do. Take me out that way, will you?"

After a startled silence she said: "All right, Steve. Come on."

"No, not together. You go first. I'll be along in a minute. And don't stand in the doorway—there could be trouble."

Dandy Jim turned to the bar, speaking to the waiting bartender. Grogan slipped the automatic from his shoulder holster and put it in the pocket of his sports coat as he got up from the booth. Keeping his hand on the gun, he walked quickly to the door marked "Private" and stepped through it. He didn't look back— his next move would be the same, whether Dandy Jim saw him or not.

Terry was waiting inside the narrow passage. The light thrown by the one bare bulb in the ceiling showed Grogan her white face looking up at him. Laughter came to them from an open doorway farther down the hall.

"Steve, what is this?"

"No time to talk now. Is that the back entrance?" He nodded toward the door at the end of the hall.

"Yes, but ..."

"Thanks, kid. I'll see you tomorrow. Don't mention this, will you?"

Grogan started down the hall, his hand still in his pocket. He bumped into a girl stepping out of the room from which he had heard the laughter. Beyond noticing that she was half-dressed and genuinely startled, he paid no attention to her, and scarcely heard the volley of profanity she sent after him.

He opened the back door and went out, moving as quickly as possible without actually running, until he was beyond the circle of light thrown by the globe hanging over the doorway. Then he paused and looked behind him for the first time. No stir of movement came from the building he had just left.

Between the cabanas to the north he could see the lights of the pool, located inside the horseshoe of the principal group of buildings. He could hear the talk and the laughter of the people around the pool. A very high-class motel, he had thought when he first came, only to find that the Casa Carillon was several cuts below the sumptuous best in the area. Rocco had chosen well, after all.

Grogan walked rapidly toward the second row of larger dwellings located at the back of the horseshoe. The parking lot at his left was well lit; the playground just beyond it was, at eleven o'clock at night, dark.

Most of the cabanas in his row were dark. This wasn't really the season—at least half of them were unoccupied. His own was dark, too. It looked brooding and forbidding in the faint moonlight, not the safe haven it had seemed when he first saw it. The gun was out of his pocket, cradled ready in his hand, and he had to restrain himself to keep from breaking into a run.

Twenty feet from the front porch a flat, soft voice said: "Easy, boy."

Grogan put the gun away as he stepped up to the porch. It was darker there, shaded by the vines, and he could barely make out Rocco's slim form getting up from the hammock.

"What's the trouble?"

"Dandy Jim came into the bar. Dandy Jim DeCarlo."

"He spot you?" Rocco's voice, still low, was more alive.

"I don't know. I came out the back way, quick. Damnit . . ."

"Take it easy, Steve. I'll drift up and keep an eye on him. You better wake Vic and plant yourself outside here."

There wasn't anything else to say. They had talked it all out, long ago. Rocco touched his shoulder, a brief gesture of reassurance, and was gone. Grogan went inside the cabana.

He moved through the living room, which was lighted only by the streak of light shining from the open door of the bath at the back of the hall. Heavy draperies kept that streak from being visible from the outside. Grogan shivered with a chill caused by more than the air conditioning. He walked to one of the bedrooms and called through the half-open door.

"Vic."

The woman's answer came almost immediately, unfogged by any remnant of sleep.

"Yes, Steve."

"Better get up. One of the boys just showed at the bar. Rocco's gone up to look around."

"Is Betsy . . ."

"Everything is all right. I'll look in at her, and then go back outside. He probably doesn't even know we're here. But I'd feel better to have you in with Betsy."

"Of course, Steve." Grogan heard the rasp of the bedsprings.

He opened the door of the next bedroom and stepped

inside. The night light was on here. It showed him the small form curled in one of the twin beds, a rag doll encircled protectively by an arm. The fair curls clung damply to Betsy's forehead. She was murmuring to herself, apparently at some pleasant memory, as she slept.

Grogan felt the choking desperation rising in his chest. Had he been a fool to bring her? He couldn't forget what she had said when she first saw the room.

"Of course I like it here." Her three-year-old treble had been self-assured. "With all my friends with me, and my own daddy in the very next bed, I'll be as safe as I was at home."

CHAPTER 2

Vic was standing in the front room when Grogan came out. She was a medium-sized woman of around thirty, not fat, but with solid flesh built over a substantial bone structure. Her hair was pulled back tightly and her high cheekbones gleamed with cold cream. She wore a green chenille robe belted at the waist; she was barefooted. The right-hand pocket of her robe sagged under the weight of its contents.

"Is she asleep?" Vic asked.

"Sure. I don't think this is it, Vic. I'm just nervous. Would you stay in with her for a while?"

"Of course." She put a hand on his arm, her strong fingers squeezing a little. "Try not to worry so much. We'll look after Betsy."

Grogan waited until she had gone into the back bedroom and shut the door. Then he picked up the phone and dialed.

"Yeah? Mallory speaking." The voice on the wire was fogged with sleep.

"Grogan."

"Trouble, Steve?" Mallory was fully awake immediately.

"I'm not sure. Dandy Jim DeCarlo is out front now, in the bar. I don't know whether he spotted me or not. What's he doing in town, Mallory?"

"I haven't had a report on him. He must be since my time. Who is he?"

"One of Henderson's boys. Not the biggest, but not the smallest, either. There's no paper out on him. Still, he's well enough known that he won't get suspicious if you pick him up to see what he's doing here."

"Right. I'll have a car there in five minutes."

Grogan crossed the room to the television set. Reaching behind it, he pulled out a double-barreled shotgun. He broke the gun to check the load and snapped it shut again with one quick motion. He dropped a flashlight into his left-hand pocket.

At the door he listened for a moment, then slipped outside. Again he paused, waiting until his eyes adjusted to the moonless night. He could hear nothing except the shouts from the pool and the hum of cars on the highway. Satisfied, he stepped off the porch, his rubber-soled shoes making no sound.

He circled the cabana, taking his time, stopping occasionally to listen. The cabins across the graveled walk, and those on either side of his own, were dark. Three doors to the north a light had come on and he could hear low-voiced conversation.

At the front of the house Grogan stopped at the porch again and picked up one of the canvas chairs sitting there. He carried it back down to the grass and placed it in the angle made by the porch and the front wall of the house. Then he seated himself and waited, shotgun across his knees. His eyes were becoming more accustomed to the gloom, but he could still see no more than the dark shapes of the cabanas on either side and in front.

Presently footsteps scraped on the graveled walk. Not stealthy steps, but someone walking hesitantly. Grogan stood up and rested the barrel of the shotgun against the porch pillar with his thumb lying lightly on the safety.

"Hello," he said.

"Steve. Steve, is that you?" Terry's voice.

"Yes. You alone?"

"Of course I'm alone. I want to talk to you."

Without waiting for a reply she left the path and crossed the grass to him. Grogan pushed the metal of the shotgun back among the vines.

"Sorry to run out on you without explaining," he said.

"Are you in trouble, Steve?" She was breathless, and sounded frightened.

"No more than usual."

Grogan didn't like to be short with her, but he wanted her out of there. He couldn't afford to stand around talking—he needed to be listening. Her next words relaxed him somewhat.

"That man at the bar—the one who came in just before you left. He's gone now. Two prowl car officers came in and he went away with them."

"Was there any trouble?"

"No. They just talked for a minute. Steve, is it the police? Do you need to get away from here?"

Grogan heard footsteps on the path again, confident,

straight-forward footsteps. And two bars of a popular tune, whistled off-key. Rocco. Grogan raised his voice slightly.

"Just a minute, Terry," he said. "I'll walk back with you."

Rocco approached them. "Hello, Steve," he said. "Evening, Miss Kelley."

"I'm going to stroll home with Terry." Grogan reached for the shotgun and pressed it into Rocco's hand as they passed. "Goodnight."

"Goodnight, Steve. Goodnight, Miss Kelley."

Terry's response was faint. She walked close beside Grogan as they went up the path. Out of earshot of the cabana she spoke softly.

"You needn't take time with me, Steve. I know you're . . ."

"I'm in no hurry now. There are a couple of things I should explain. Could we drop into your place for a cup of coffee?"

Grogan didn't want to explain, not to her or anyone else. Too many people were in on it now. Still, he couldn't leave her quite as curious as she must be at the moment. Better to trust her with a little of it than to have her speculating about him, and maybe talking.

"Sure," she said, her voice less taut. "The condemned man at least has time for a cup of coffee, is that it?"

"Something like that."

Terry's cabin, just behind the main building, was one of the smallest in the establishment. Grogan had never been inside before. When she snapped on the light, he stood in a bed-sitting room with a kitchenette in one corner, and a closed door at the far side. Without conscious thought Grogan crossed the room and pulled the curtains shut.

Terry tossed her short coat across the back of a chair. She was still wearing the black dress in which she sang. She looked up at Grogan, trying to smile, obviously frightened, and his heart went out to her.

"Is it the police?" she asked again. "I have an old car, Steve, that nobody would recognize. If you need it...."

Grogan grinned at her. "Do you make a habit of helping fugitives, lady?"

"I thought it was about the little girl, and...."

"Betsy is my daughter," Grogan said. The grin was gone.

"Oh, I know she is, Steve. I thought perhaps it was divorce trouble, or something like that."

"The police aren't after me, Terry. At least not yet." Grogan sank into an armchair and stretched his long legs in front of him. "I'd like to tell you something about it, if you want to hear." Her quick offer of assistance had touched him.

"Only if you want to tell me. Should I make the coffee?"

"Skip the coffee. Unless you want some."

Terry laughed, shakily. "Not really. Not on top of the champagne."

"First," Grogan said, "it would help for you to tell me what you have been thinking about me—about all of us. I want to know if there has been any gossip."

Terry sat down in a straight chair. It was across the room from Grogan, but the place was so small they were only a few feet apart. She caught her lower lip between white teeth and thought about it.

"I don't think there has been any gossip, Steve. Naturally, it is an unusual arrangement, just you and the little girl with Mr. and Mrs. Rocco. I have probably noticed more than anyone else because . . . well, just because. I have wondered if you were afraid someone would try to take Betsy, because you watch her so carefully. Usually she isn't out of your sight. If she is, one or both of the Roccos is always there."

"So you thought?"

"I thought you might have taken her from her mother, after a divorce, and the law might be after you."

"You would help me do that?"

"I guess I would. I don't know anything about her mother, of course. I've watched Betsy with you, though, and she wouldn't be happy away from you. You make it plain that her welfare is about your only interest." She smiled slightly. "I never really figured you for my butter-and-egg man, Steve. 'No stepmother' stands out all over your attitude."

Grogan sighed. "I didn't know it was so plain. I could be wrong about that—I've been wrong about a lot of things. But I had a stepmother myself. That isn't what I want to talk to you about, though. It's nothing like you think. Betsy's mother is dead. She died when Betsy was born."

"Steve, I . . ."

"It's all right. That's a long time ago now. A man gets used to anything. This trouble is something entirely different."

"You needn't tell me."

"I want to. I'm a cop, Terry. At least I have been a cop, most of my life. I'm on indefinite leave now. I met Lynn—Betsy's mother—on a case. Her aunt had been murdered. The aunt was a very wealthy woman, and left the money to Lynn. When Lynn died, it came to me. The money hasn't anything to do with my troubles, except that it gives me a chance to handle things differently than I would otherwise. Maybe better, maybe worse. I don't know."

"I know you do the best you can, Steve." She was obviously sorry for him.

"Oh, sure. Anyway, a couple of months ago I broke a case, a very big case. Dope syndicate. The lines ran way up, as far up as a respectable businessman we had never even suspected. He got away from us and he's hiding out now, but it's just a matter of time."

Grogan paused for a moment, regretting the past. Damn his pride, or whatever it was, that kept him at work with the force. Dread of boredom, really, was what it had been. He wasn't cut out for a rich idler— he had no hobbies or sources of amusement. He had stayed on, and it had brought Betsy to this.

"My testimony is the key. If I don't go on the stand, he might get away with it. At least he wouldn't burn, because only I can tie him up with murder. If I go on the stand and change my story a little, a very little, he could go scot-free. That's where the rub comes in."

"Oh, Steve. Betsy...."

"That's right: Betsy. A stoolie tipped me off. They were thinking of snatching her, to make me change my tune. I'm too crazy about her. The word got around."

"Steve, what a dreadful choice."

Grogan looked at her, surprised. "Choice? It was no choice at all." Some of the suppressed violence crept into his voice, roughening it. "Between Betsy and what is called 'the good of society', I wouldn't need long to think it over. The trouble is, I could never trust them. I ran for it."

"And you think you were traced here?"

"I'm always on the lookout for them to trace me

anywhere. It's a big organization—I can't hope to stay out of sight forever."

Terry looked frightened, and ready to cry. "Steve, it's so horrible. I see now there is nothing I can . . ."

"You can help me a lot by not talking about tonight. Maybe you can smooth over the deal with that girl I ran into back by the dressing room."

"I already have. I told her you made a pass at me in the hall, and were mad because I slapped you."

"Good girl. Well, you must be due to go on pretty soon. I'd better be getting back."

"Steve, I know you have more experience at this sort of thing than I have, but were you wise to come out here? Couldn't the police have protected you?"

Grogan stood up. "Who knows what's wise? I only know Betsy is mine, all mine, and I figure I can look after her better than anyone else can. Go on back to work, kid. Sorry to mix you up in my troubles."

He felt very alone as he walked back toward the cabana. Sure, it would have been comforting to have the department around him. He could have holed up just the same in the city, with Rocco and Vic, and the boys would have kept a couple of cruisers circling the block all the time. It would have been just as safe, perhaps, up to the point of the trial.

Grogan shivered. That was why he felt so all alone. He had been an honest cop all his life. Not much else, maybe, but an honest cop. Now it was different. Every man has his price, Grogan had always heard, and now he knew it to be true. Betsy's safety was his price.

It meant turning back on all he had stood for, but Grogan didn't want to stay where the department could put its hand on him when Henderson came up for trial. He had no intention of getting on that stand

and giving testimony that might sign Betsy's death warrant. And he hadn't told Terry all of it, either. Not the part which made his policeman's conscience writhe most painfully. About the ledger sheets the dying man had passed to him. The sheets Henderson had to regain if he were ever to operate safely again even after Grogan was dead. They were at once Grogan's ace in the hole and his weak point. While he had them, Henderson would walk warily, except to try to get his hands on Betsy for bargaining. Henderson swore that if Grogan turned them over to the department he would have Betsy killed, and Grogan believed that in a final grasp for revenge Henderson would do just that.

CHAPTER 3

Grogan called Mallory again, this time dialing headquarters.

"Anything out of line?"

"He's just an innocent tourist. He's a tourist packing a gun without a permit, though, and I can hang on to him for quite a while."

Grogan thought it over, holding the receiver negligently and leaving the line quiet. Abruptly he made up his mind. "Turn him loose, Bill. Hold him twenty minutes more and turn him loose. Without a tail."

"Listen, Steve, I can't . . ."

"You just do it. What happens after that is no skin off your nose. You won't know a thing about it. Turn him loose in twenty minutes, Bill."

Grogan cradled the phone without waiting for

further argument. Anger was boiling inside his chest, almost replacing the icy terror he had carried for so long. He had cowered enough in the shadows—it was time to show that the hunted rabbit had teeth of its own. He looked up at Rocco, who had followed him inside the house.

"What now, Steve?"

Vic had come out of the bedroom and stood silently watching them. Without make-up she was not pretty; her face was almost plain, except for the beauty of the gravely anxious eyes.

Grogan didn't answer. He took off his coat and unbuckled the shoulder harness holding his automatic. He looked at it disdainfully before he tossed it to the chair. A hell of a poor way to carry a gun. He went to the bedroom and rummaged in his suitcase, his hands fumbling and awkward because his attention was on the small figure in the bed. When Betsy sighed in her sleep and turned over, he felt a chill down his spine.

He returned to the front room carrying his short-barreled .38 revolver and its belt holster. He fastened the holster in place while the other two watched.

Vic said: "Steve, you mustn't do anything rash. You simply mustn't."

"I don't consider this rash. I'm just going to show the boys they aren't playing the safest game in the world."

"But, Steve...."

Rocco touched her shoulder, quieting her. "It's for Steve to decide," he said. "You want me along?"

"No, thanks. You keep the home fires burning."

Vic said: "You will be careful, Steve? It won't help for you to get hurt."

Grogan checked his irritation with the thought that she had a right to her opinion. Vic was vitally concerned in all of this, and she wasn't speaking for herself, anyway. He caught her elbows and pulled her closer to him.

"I'll be careful. I'm not just going off on a blind tear. I figure this is good business. These are rats we're dealing with—they may not be so brave if they get a lesson on the facts of life."

Vic's smile lit her plain features and brought them alive. She raised her mouth to him; Grogan bent down and kissed her briefly. He was suddenly conscious of Rocco's dark, expressionless features.

He forgot them both as soon as he closed the front door behind him. There wasn't room in his mind for anything but Betsy, and the problems connected with keeping her alive and well. And, if possible, untouched by the terror of all of this.

Grogan took the graveled path to the parking lot. One of the advantages of this place was that cars could not drive to the cabana. Recollection of that brought Rocco into his consciousness again. Rocco had chosen well when he picked the hideout. Grogan was never sure of Rocco's exact attitude toward Vic, or of his attitude toward Vic and Grogan together, but there was no doubt of his feelings for Betsy. That was the important thing—he would trust her safety to Rocco as willingly as he would trust it to any man alive.

Grogan got the Olds headed for town at a steady sixty. There was no rush—he had time enough. He had told Mallory twenty minutes and he knew he could count on that. Bill didn't like it very well, not in his own town, but he owed Grogan that much. Bill Mallory could be counted on to pay his debts. Grogan didn't even feel embarrassment at the thought. He had never been much for collecting that kind of debt, but Betsy's danger changed all the rules.

Grogan didn't discount the danger to himself in what he was about to do. He didn't consider it unimportant, either, as he would have four years before. Having a three-year-old dependent on you as the only parent can change the values. For the first time in his life Grogan was shaping his conduct with an eye to his personal safety, because his survival was necessary for Betsy.

No, he had to be careful. They weren't out to kill him, because Grogan dead wasn't the answer they wanted. They had gotten the word that the ledger would turn up with his death. A Grogan who failed to show at the trial would be better, and a Grogan who would say what they wanted him to say because his daughter was in their hands would be best of all. But if he pushed them too hard, put them in immediate fear of their own physical safety, then of course these hired guns would kill if they could.

Grogan parked the Olds half a block from the entrance to the police station, on the same side of the street. At midnight the town was brilliantly lit, and there was more activity on the streets than during the day. He didn't like the character of the people on the sidewalks. Too many tourists, too shifting a population, for the police ever to be sure just who was in town. On the other side of the picture there was Mallory. It was Mallory's town, and he could be counted on to use the weight of the police force to give Grogan the sort of help he wanted without tying him up officially when Grogan had other ideas. Nothing was ever perfect, but Mallory tipped the balance.

Grogan stiffened to attention as Dandy Jim DeCarlo came out the front door of the police station and stood for a moment on the sidewalk. He wasn't quite so at ease as he had been in the bar of the Casa Carillon. Tough as he was, and contemptuous of the law, Dandy Jim hadn't liked being pulled into the station and he wasn't happy about standing there in front of it. All that showed in the defiant swagger of his shoulders and the quick, darting glances he sent over the crowd on the sidewalk. Then he beckoned to a cruising cab.

The cab went directly to a small motel on the outskirts of town. Not one of the big, neon-splashed jobs; not even approaching the spurious splendor of the Casa Carillon. It was just a roadside spot where a tourist without much money would pull in for the night. Dandy Jim would never have chosen such a place unless he was trying to stay under cover. Grogan parked the Olds and was close behind DeCarlo by the time his man finished paying off the cab.

Grogan said: "Hello, Jim."

The street was deserted. The motel behind them was dark, even the office was closed for the night. They were alone under a bright street light. Naked fear glistened on DeCarlo's thin cheeks as he turned to Grogan.

"Been looking for me?" Grogan asked.

"Looking for you? No, Christ, no. Why would I look for you?"

Grogan took a step closer. "Don't start out by lying to me," he said softly. "Whether you get off this spot depends on not lying to me. Get that through your head, Jim."

"I don't even have a gun." DeCarlo's voice, always before so full of cynical assurance, was high and a little thin. "Those lousy cops kept it."

Grogan laughed. "You think I mind that? If I decide you're more good to me dead, Jim, I won't make a sporting proposition out of it. No gun suits me just fine."

"What do you want with me?"

"I want to know who is in town with you. And where."

DeCarlo's glance darted up and down the street. There was nothing to give him reassurance. Grogan took another step and gripped his arm.

"Talk."

"All right. Kicker Jenson and Tony Small are with me. Back there in cabin seven. But we don't have anything to do with . . ."

"Shut up and lead the way. They both in there?"

"I think so. Christ, you're hurting my arm."

"I may decide to break it. Is Kicker high tonight?"

"I don't think so. I can't be sure, though. I haven't seen him for a couple of hours. You, know how it is, Grogan—I can't be sure."

"Let's go in and see them." Grogan kept his paralyzing grip on the arm. "I don't know what signals you guys have, and don't much care. This gun will be on you when we go in, and if there's trouble, you're first."

As they approached number seven Grogan shifted his grip to DeCarlo's shoulder, near the collar. The .38 was in his right hand. Light shone from the window of the cabin.

DeCarlo rapped on the flimsy wooden door. "It's me," he said. His voice sounded normal, but Grogan could feel the quiver of muscles under his finger.

"Okay. Just a minute."

The door opened, and Grogan pushed DeCarlo ahead

of him as they stepped inside. The heavy-set, swarthy man who faced them grunted in surprise as he recognized Grogan and froze into immobility at the gun covering him over DeCarlo's shoulder. Another man was lying on the opened-out couch which had been made into a bed in the front room. An automatic rested on a table beside the bed.

"Reach for it if you feel lucky, Kicker," Grogan said. He kicked the door shut with his heel.

Kicker Jenson remained motionless on the bed. He was small, much smaller than DeCarlo. Dressed only in shorts and undershirt which exposed his pasty skin and flabby muscles, he looked even more unimposing than Grogan remembered him. There was no indication of dope in him at the moment, though he must have had a fairly recent fix to have his nerves under such good control.

"I'm no gambler," Kicker said. "What you want with us, copper?"

The sight of the three of them together, symbolizing all the problems which were haunting him, sent Grogan's anger boiling over. He gripped DeCarlo's collar more firmly and slammed him into Tony Small, standing just in front of them, with such force that the two men rocketed back against the wall. DeCarlo fell to the floor from the impact; Small, more solidly built, leaned on the wall and shook his head to clear it from the effect of having it smashed against the woodwork. He made no move toward the gun hanging in a shoulder harness over his gaudy sport shirt.

"We know you're a big man, copper," Kicker Jenson said. "What was that for?"

"Get over there with your pals."

Grogan watched while they ranged themselves along

the wall. DeCarlo, on his feet now, was breathing in quick, uneven gasps. The big Small still shook his head, but more slowly. Jenson tried to look nonchalant.

"You want me to take this gun off?" Small asked.

"I don't give a damn what you do with the gun. Try to use it, and I won't have any trouble making up my mind."

Silence stretched out, bleak and ugly. The little room, without air conditioning, was muggily hot. Grogan watched the beads of sweat form on the features of the three men as they shifted uneasily.

Jenson finally spoke. "You got nothing on us, copper," he said.

"That's your big mistake, you louse," Grogan said. "You're thinking of me as a cop, going by cop's rules. I'm not, anymore. I'm a father, and you three rats are fooling around my kid. I'm just trying to decide whether the lot of you will be a better warning if I leave you dead in this room, or if I let you pass the word on how I'm playing it from now on."

He saw from their faces that they believed him. Grogan himself wasn't entirely sure. With his anger under control, he doubted his ability to shoot them down as they stood there, unless one of them made a threatening move. Probably not. Not until . . . that idea sent his fury blazing again.

Jenson, seeing his changed expression, said quickly: "I'm a good talker, lieutenant. We all are. What word do you want passed?"

"All right. Tell the boys this. I've turned wild—wilder than any of you two-bit guns can ever be. I know most of the Henderson mob, and from now on I'll shoot on sight. Stay away from me. I won't fool with proof—if I see a face I'm suspicious of, it will belong to a walking corpse right then."

"Okay, lieutenant. Sure. We'll give the word."

"And tell Henderson, personally. There are worse things than taking his chance on the chair. If my kid is harmed in any way, or even threatened again, he's signed his own death warrant. I'll hunt him down and get him if it takes the rest of my life. Not only him, but every one of you rats connected with him. Not as a cop, remember, but as a guy who won't have a thing to lose, and I'll shoot from cover like one of you would. We've changed the rules in this thing."

DeCarlo cleared his throat. "Look, lieutenant, don't get me wrong. I'm not trying to argue—what you say is good enough for me. It just seems to me it might be a good idea. You want us to offer Henderson a deal?"

There it was, out in the open, the question which had been dogging Grogan's conscience. Would he, for the sake of one trusting three-year-old, let Henderson's evil go unchecked? It was an awful price, one he couldn't cancel out even by killing Henderson later, because that wouldn't break up the syndicate. But it was a question he didn't have to answer yet. Even if he were willing, a deal with Henderson would be meaningless, because Henderson couldn't be trusted.

"I've told you the deal," Grogan said. "Let me alone. That's Henderson's best chance of keeping me off that stand. Just let me alone."

"Sure, lieutenant. We'll tell him."

Grogan studied the three men ranged against the wall. Tony Small, wooden-faced and stolid, his fear showing only in his eyes. Jenson, perfectly quiet and expressionless, but being very careful to make no untoward movement. DeCarlo, plainly scared to death. He knew none of them would give him trouble tonight.

Grogan backed to the door. "Then we understand each other. The next man who has trouble with me has it all the way. And tell Henderson something else. I'm leaving a will. If something happens to me, Rocco will be on the prowl for you just as I am. Think it over."

CHAPTER 4

Grogan drove back to the Casa Carillon. With anger gone his nerves were jumping again. This hadn't done any good—hadn't changed a thing. He might scare out the small-timers but he knew he wouldn't be able to scare Henderson permanently. Henderson couldn't afford to scare, because he was a dead man if Grogan got on that stand and told the truth.

He had, at best, gained himself a little time, while Henderson figured his next step. Time to plot his course here, or to run again. Any way he figured his thoughts went around in a circle and came back to the small, defenseless figure of Betsy. Grogan felt old and tired when he parked the Olds at the motor court.

He whistled as he approached the darkened cabin. Rocco stepped out of the shadows of the porch to meet him and they went inside together. Grogan snapped the switch beside the door. The flooding light showed them Vic sitting in an armchair on the far side of the room, her small pistol lying beside her hand.

"Steve," she said, her voice low. "You're back safe."

Grogan sat down. He wanted to scream and swear and break the furniture, and so he moved softly and quietly, keeping his face expressionless.

"Sure," he said. "I've got to stay safe, don't I?"

"How did it go?" Rocco asked.

"Not much use, I suppose. I sent word to Henderson I would kill him if anything happened to Betsy. It probably gained me a couple of days."

"You don't think they might be so frightened they won't...." Vic's voice was eager.

"No. These boys, sure. Not Henderson."

"No, not Henderson," Rocco said. "He knows you would have killed him before this if you could have gotten to him."

"There's just this little difference. I couldn't get to him before because I couldn't afford to risk his getting me, and I couldn't afford to burn for it. If anything happens to Betsy, the rules would change. Maybe that will make him think a little."

"Maybe." Rocco had remained standing beside the door, still holding the shotgun. Now he propped it against the wall. "You're the boss, Steve, but just a suggestion. Would it be any better if only two of them went back? Or one?"

Grogan shook his head. "No. Thanks, Rocco, but no. I won't make things too hot for Bill Mallory unless I'm sure it will do some good."

Vic stood up swiftly, the swirl of her robe showing her legs as she crossed the room to them. Her face was tight and she looked ready to cry.

"I think you're crazy," she said. "Both of you. You talk about killing as the answer to everything. Do you think you can kill everyone in the gang?"

She stood close to Rocco, directing the question to him. They were almost of a height as they looked at each other. Rocco smiled bleakly.

"We can try," he said. "You got any better ideas, baby?"

She turned away, biting her lip. Grogan was surprised. Vic never cried.

"I thought not," Rocco said. "I'm going out for a beer. Want to get dressed and come along, baby?"

"No." Her voice was muffled. "I want to talk to Steve."

"Okay." Rocco's glance was impersonal as he looked at Grogan. "I'll be back in an hour or so, Steve." He went out and closed the door softly behind him.

The other two did not speak for several minutes after he left. Grogan, unwilling to talk but reluctant to offend her, shifted in his chair. She turned toward him. "Steve, you've got to . . ."

"It's no good, Vic. We've said it all. Besides, I thought you were in agreement."

"Maybe I was. I can see now it's all wrong."

"What do you want me to do?"

She crossed the room and sat down in a chair pulled close to Grogan's. She put a hand on his arm, lightly and hesitantly, and then withdrew it. She was almost beautiful then in her earnestness, even without make-up and with her hair pulled back in a tight knot.

"I think you should go back, Steve. I think it would be better. For Betsy, for you, for everybody."

"You can go any time."

"You know I don't mean that." She refused to anger.

Grogan was ashamed of himself. "I know you don't. I'm sorry Vic. My nerves are shot." He put his hand over hers.

"That's what I mean, Steve. You can't go on this way forever."

"It won't be forever."

"Won't it? If you keep running, they may not bring Henderson to trial, or he may get off. Both sides will go on looking for you. Some day they will corner you.

Even if they don't, this kind of a life isn't good for Betsy. She can already tell something is wrong. Little girls don't grow up normally when they have to be watched with a gun every minute."

Grogan realized that his tightened grasp must be crushing her fingers, although she gave no indication of pain. He released her abruptly.

"At least she will grow up," he said. "The other way . . ."

"The other way isn't any more risky than this. Are you sure this isn't egotism, Steve? Wanting to do it all yourself, to prove she is yours? Go back and trust the department to look after both of you. Just until the trial—after that she will be safe."

"Or dead." Saying the word made Grogan break out in a cold sweat. He had never let himself even think that before. Not so definitely. "Not in a thousand years," he said. "I won't set her up for a target."

"She is that now, Steve. It's a bad choice, but I believe going back is the better of the two."

"You mean three," Grogan said tonelessly. "I can do what Henderson wants."

Vic sighed. "No, you can't, Steve. I could. Or Rocco. But you couldn't, not really, even though Betsy means more to you than she does to us. Or if you did, it would turn you so sour on life the result would be as bad for her in the long run. You're an honest cop, Steve. That's been your life. If you change now, and let Henderson get away with this, you'll remember it every time you see a headline about a kid caught up in the dope traffic. When a corpse is fished out of the river, you'll think of Henderson, and how you might have stopped him. It would destroy you. Then where would Betsy be?"

Grogan got up and paced across the room and back, blindly. He didn't want to listen to her, because all of the things she was saying he had thought of a hundred times, much as he tried to crowd them out of his mind.

"Look," he said. "I'm tougher than you think. This duty to society stuff is all right, but it's not the pot of gold at the end of the rainbow for me. Society has had all of me for fifteen years, and now that's out the window. Now it's Betsy. Anything I can do for her, I will do without being too damned squeamish. She's all the duty I've got, and I'm keeping her safe. Me. My own way."

"Do you think her mother . . ."

"Lynn doesn't enter into this. That's over, a long time ago. Sure, when I married her I thought it was the most wonderful miracle that ever happened to me. Me, a dumb cop with a girl like that loving me. Her money didn't count, except that I would have been more comfortable if she hadn't had it. She was the miracle, I thought, and when she died I figured it was the end of the world. Well, I was wrong on both counts."

"Steve . . ."

"Betsy was the miracle, and my world doesn't end while she is here to look after. Don't keep this kind of talk up, Vic, or we split. Right now. I mean it."

Grogan sat down again, exhausted. He was worn out. He didn't want to talk about it anymore, or even to think.

"You don't mean that, Steve." Color stood out on her high cheek bones. "I'm telling you things you need to hear. You speak of doing what Henderson wants. Do you think you could trust him? Say you sell out, turn your back on everything you have ever stood for. You go back, you get on the stand and lie. You refuse to identify Henderson. He goes free. Do you think he would let you alone after that? Let you live? What is going to happen to Betsy when Henderson finally gets you?"

There it was again. Vic was right, at least on that part of it. Henderson would never let him go while they both lived.

"You may be partly right," he said.

"I'm sure of it, Steve. Will you . . ."

"Not the way you mean. But it isn't fair to Betsy to drag it out like this. I was wrong in not pushing harder for a showdown before we left the East. Maybe I had better try to beat those boys back."

"No, Steve." Her alarm was quick. "You know you can't get to Henderson—you wouldn't have a chance. He'll be under cover with an army around him. He'd know you were coming before you got off the plane. Then what about Betsy?"

"I wouldn't be that much of a cinch to lose. And even if I did, the heat would be off her. She would have you and Rocco. And Lynn's money."

Vic laughed, a bitter, strained sound entirely without humor. "A wonderful life that would be. An ex-cop with a wife who will never divorce him and a carnival sharpshooter whose past stands out all over her. You're wishing that on your daughter?"

The weight of it pressed in on Grogan. Vic and Rocco. Good-hearted people, his kind of people, the sort he had been used to all his life. He seldom thought much about their relationship. But for Betsy to grow up with only them? She was so much like her mother. He had spoken of Lynn as being in the past, and usually he could think of her that way, but she came back to him then. She had moved across the tracks to marry him, in a sense, but they had built a life of their own. One that Vic and Rocco could fit into casually but not as guardians for her daughter. His face must have disclosed his thoughts.

"You see?" Vic said. Sadly, and with the bitterness gone. "I would do anything for Betsy, Steve. Give up Rocco, of course. Anything. But that wouldn't be the answer. I'm not the one to raise a child like that."

"Vic . . ."

"It's nothing to talk about. We both see it. And an old maid governess or a swank school isn't the answer either. She needs you and a normal home and an end to this life. You'll have to marry again, Steve. Some nice girl with nothing to forget, like Liza Carrol next door. She can be a credit to Betsy and the other children you will have. You have to plan for that."

Grogan's astonishment momentarily overrode his other emotions. Liza Carrol, the good-looking blond widow who had moved into the cabin beside them shortly after their own arrival, had never given him the slightest reason to suspect she could be romantically interested in him. Liza was friendly and obviously fond of Betsy, but that was all. She was, he was willing to concede, very beautiful, and out of the top drawer socially. But she didn't figure in his present plans.

"You paint a pretty picture," Grogan said. He knew his short laugh was ugly. "All I've got to do is get married and pretend this never happened. For God's sake, Vic!"

Grogan pulled a cigarette from his pocket and lit it. Dragging deeply on the smoke, he weighed the lighter in his hand and studied it because he didn't want to make his mind face anything else. It was an expensive bauble, one that would have cost a couple of months' pay in the old days. He would still never buy a useless toy like that for himself. It had been a birthday present from Lynn. He kept it because of that.

A couple of months' pay. God, what a long time ago that seemed. It was farther away than his life as a kid, because Betsy brought that back to him daily. He never looked at her but that he thought of his old man, the bum, and the frowzy stepmother who had batted him around. He looked at her and thought how things were going to be different with her.

Different not just because of her mother's money but because he, Grogan, wasn't going to bat her around and wasn't going to turn her over to any stepmother and was going to damn well look after her.

All that money. Once he would have figured it as the answer to any problem. Again that was as a kid. Just give him money, he had thought, and he would show that lousy neighborhood. Now he had the money and it couldn't do a thing for him. He became conscious that Vic was still talking.

". . . can't try to fight him alone," she was saying. "He has taken it easy so far, hoping to bring you into his corner. Once he gives up on that there'll be a price on your head big enough to have every gunman in the country after you. You know what a man like that can buy with the money he is willing to spend, Steve."

Grogan's full attention snapped back to the present. He stared at Vic, sitting there talking earnestly to him. Her face was faintly flushed. Grogan smiled at her.

"Yeah," he said, "I know. I was forgetting for a while, but you're right all the way. A man can buy a lot with money."

He got up and crossed the room to the telephone. Mallory's home number again. Bill would be getting a little tired of this, but he would still go along. Mallory's voice was thick with sleep when he at length answered the phone.

"Just one more favor, Bill," Grogan said. "The last one, I hope."

"Name it."

"I had a visit with our friend DeCarlo in the Roseland Motel. He's holed up there with a couple of pals—a big yegg named Tony Small and a little hophead they call Kicker Jenson. I want to talk to Jenson by himself. Will you pick up DeCarlo again, and Small along with him? A couple of hours will be enough."

A long pause. Then: "What's on your mind, Steve?"

"Nothing to worry you. I won't hurt Jenson, if that's troubling you. His own mother couldn't treat him any more gentle than I'm going to."

"All right, Steve."

"Fine. Make it in just thirty minutes, will you?"

Grogan hung up the receiver and turned to Vic. She was watching him with a worried frown.

"Steve, what are you going to do?"

"I'm getting smart for a change," Grogan said. "I'm going to find out what I can buy with a little money."

CHAPTER 5

Grogan approached the door of cabin number seven at the Roseland Motel, careful to make no noise, and rapped lightly.

"Now what?" Jenson's answer was immediate.

"It's me," Grogan said. "No names, Kicker."

"What the hell do you want?"

"Just a little talk. Open the door and stand in the light for a minute, Kicker."

"Why should I?"

"You want me to shove the door in and drag you out?"

"All right, all right."

The door opened and Kicker Jenson stood framed in the light. He had on a pair of trousers, but was still barefooted and wore only an undershirt over his scrawny chest. He held both hands in front of him, emphasizing their emptiness. Grogan shouldered him aside and walked in, closing the door behind him.

"Why are you back again?" Jenson asked.

Grogan settled himself in a chair by the door. This errand put a bad taste in his mouth, but he ignored it. This was something he had to do.

"I wanted a little talk with you, Kicker," he said. "I needed your pals out of the way so I had them picked up."

"Just like that, huh? Are you the law in this town, too?"

"Better than the law. I've got the law doing what I want. Keep that in mind, if you ever take it in your head to cross me."

Jenson sneered. Grogan was pleased to see that the little man's spirit wasn't broken by all this. He was holding still for it because there was nothing else to do at the moment, but he was something less than scared to death. That made him better for Grogan's purpose.

"Cross you in what, for God's sake?" Jenson asked. "I told you I was laying off, and I meant it. I can't get out of town until morning."

"I've got a proposition to make you," Grogan said. "You think I went to all this trouble to get Tony and DeCarlo out of the way because I like your company?"

Jenson shrugged. "So now we're in business together. You going to tell me about it?"

"That's right."

"So go ahead. You got the dice."

Grogan didn't enjoy putting it into words. This was a sorry specimen in front of him, surveyed from any angle, but he was the best choice available. Dandy Jim DeCarlo didn't have the steel in him for what Grogan wanted, and Tony Small didn't have the brains. Jenson had guts and he wasn't stupid. On the other side of the scales was the fact that he was a hophead and therefore entirely unreliable, but Grogan had already considered all of that and made his pick. You worked with the tools at hand.

"This isn't for your pals to hear about," Grogan said. "It's just between you and me. They've got no way of knowing I ever came to see you."

"Go ahead." If Jenson was interested, he gave no sign.

"I'm not a cop now, Kicker. I'm a private citizen, with a hell of a lot of money. I suppose you know all about that."

"Is this the story of your life?" Jenson could sense that Grogan was not so menacing as he had been earlier in the evening.

"Don't get smart. I'll give you this deal just once. If you aren't interested say so and I'll shop around somewhere else, but you keep it quiet. One whisper about this and you're dead, Kicker."

"Okay, okay. I'm no squealer."

"I want a chore done. When it is, and I've got the

proof, I'll have a hundred grand for you. A hundred grand, Kicker, in real money. Not phony. Not hot. It'll buy one hundred cents on the dollar. It's your chance to make a stake you never dreamed of getting your hands on."

The cluttered little room was quiet, disturbed only by Kicker Jenson's suddenly rasping breath. Grogan let him think about it for a long moment.

"And you'll be dealing with Steve Grogan," Grogan said.

"You know me, you've known about me for years. You know my word's good for the money. I was an honest cop when the money was all around me for the asking. Have you got any doubts I'll pay off?"

Jenson shook his head. He rubbed his palms together in a quick, nervous motion, and Grogan saw they were sweating. The little hophead licked his lips, his tongue darting in and out in snakelike motions.

"I guess I know what the chore is," he said softly.

"Yeah, I guess you do. You can get to Henderson, Kicker, real easy, because he'll want a report from you. I want Henderson dead."

CHAPTER 6

Three thousand miles away, Marcus Henderson sat in his hideout hotel room and thought about Grogan with the same intensity with which Grogan considered him. Grogan, Grogan. Every avenue he turned to was blocked by Grogan, as had been the case since the big policeman turned up on his trail a year before. Henderson said: "Damn Grogan to Hell."

Charley Norris, lying relaxed on the sofa, tossed his

magazine to the floor. When he spoke his voice carried the mockery which was beginning to wear on Henderson's nerves.

"Grogan is important, all right," Norris said. "You're making him more so. I've told you before, the thing to do now is leave him alone. You've scared him out of town, and he has kept his mouth shut on the records. That's all you can hope for. Without that ledger the D. A. won't know where to start; with it he can trace every shipment through the company. You were a fool to . . ."

"Watch that 'fool' talk."

Henderson felt the muscles of his neck tense with the old familiar fury. He forced himself to pause. Mustn't let it take possession of him. That had been the beginning of this trouble, even more than Grogan's prying. Once he suspected Smiley had been a stool for Grogan, he had let the rage push him into a shooting, even though he knew Grogan was prowling the outer office. A shooting that was not instantly fatal, giving Smiley time to talk to Grogan and in one last malicious burst of revenge give him the ledger that would lead them so surely to all the witnesses. It was in code, but the code would never stand up under the scrutiny of police experts. It had been a bad mistake.

In control of himself again, Henderson took some satisfaction from the pasty hue of Norris's complexion. Charley was remembering, too, and knew he had gone too far. It diverted Henderson to get beneath that mask of smug respectability and show Norris he was not personally safe in this game he played with such amusement. At the same time, while Charley controlled the dummy corporation, it wouldn't do to push him too far. Giving Norris that much power might have been another mistake.

"I'm just keeping an eye on him," Henderson said. "When the boys get back . . ."

Norris swung his feet to the floor and sat up. He was a medium-sized man, about Henderson's own height, but with flabby muscles and stooped shoulders which contrasted with Henderson's lean fitness. Norris's smooth, clever features were worried.

"I don't like it," he said. "We shouldn't keep pushing him. I don't know how far you can trust the boys on a thing like this."

"I've got to keep him in sight. If he once figures he has completely lost us, he'll get over being scared. And I'm a trusting soul, Charley. Look how far I trust you."

They studied each other with no illusions at all, though both expressions were carefully masked. Henderson had never been contented with the arrangement which left his getaway money so much in Norris's control, but he had needed the front. The supposedly successful corporation lawyer, his gambling debts unknown outside the underworld, made an excellent cover. But it was getting time to end it.

"Sure," Norris said, "we trust each other. What about Babe? I thought you trusted her, too, but I haven't seen her around for a few days."

"She's with Grogan. I want to know if the boys do try to cross me."

Norris shook his head, dissatisfied. "I think it's a mistake," he said. "You're pushing Grogan too hard. I don't see any percentage in it. God knows you've taken enough trouble building this up for a fadeout. If you're going to do it, do it now, and forget Grogan."

"Maybe you're right," Henderson said easily. "I think

it's time to cash in the holdings. You take your share, I take mine, and we go our ways."

That was going to be the ticklish point, of course. There had never been real trust between them. Norris felt safe only while he controlled the purse strings through the dummy corporation, and Henderson was protected from a double-cross only by the physical fear he inspired in the lawyer. Henderson got up and stood in front of the mirror.

He studied his changed reflection with pleased concentration. The gleaming bald head, which made him look years older than the hair piece he had worn through his years as 'Henderson'. So many years he even thought of himself by that name. Now his skin was pale, scrubbed clean at last of the dark makeup he had so faithfully applied. The plain, rimless glasses gave him an almost scholarly look. He was a different man.

"All right," Norris said. "I'll fix it up. In the meantime, for God's sake, lay off Grogan."

Henderson only smiled at him. He was almost tempted to let Charley further into his thought processes to prove how well he had this scheme worked out. Kicker Jenson and the boys were under strict orders to harm neither Grogan nor the child, but to stir him up, worry him. Make him so desperate he would stop running and try to strike back at Henderson.

Henderson, nervous in spite of himself, did not like that idea too well, but it had to be. Just disappearing was not enough. Someday, somehow, they might link him up. He had to die, so the hunt would end. It would be more believable if his death could be blamed on Grogan.

Talking it over with Charley would have been helpful, because that slippery, conniving brain was an asset in making any plan; but Charley himself was part of the plan. He was the same general size as Henderson and, also like Henderson, his fingerprints were not on record. He had no family and there was no one to miss him or sound an alarm if he disappeared. Once they had split the loot it would be safer for Henderson to have him dead. It would be perfect to have him identified as Henderson.

"I should be hearing from Kicker any time, now," Henderson said.

"Kicker Jenson? My God, you aren't using that hophead on anything connected with Grogan, are you?"

Henderson controlled his irritation. He himself was none too satisfied with the choice, but it had been a balancing of the assets. He had picked Jenson because he thought the little man would be most likely to listen to any proposition Grogan might make him. And because he was confident of his own ability to keep Jenson from carrying through.

The phone rang and Norris crossed the room to answer it. Henderson felt satisfaction in the knowledge that the call would be for Charley; this was Charley's room, booked in his name. There was nothing to tie Henderson to it. Only Charley knew he was here.

Henderson listened to Norris's end of the conversation, and felt excitement rising. Norris said: "All right, I think I can. It will be a couple of hours before I reach him. I'll call you back."

"Jenson?" Henderson asked.

"That's right. He wants to see you. Says it won't

keep."

Henderson took off the rimless glasses and stood up. He felt better, now that the time was near. He loosened his collar and began to spread the dark lotion over his features, while Charley Norris watched broodingly.

An hour later Henderson was able to look in the mirror with satisfaction at what he saw. The change was incredible, even to him who had accomplished it step by step. The hair piece altered the naked outline of his skull; the lotion made his features swarthy, almost heavy. The contact lenses gave him a faintly bug-eyed appearance. The sharply cut suit was a contrast to the dowdy blue serge of his other characterization.

"It's pretty good," Norris said grudgingly.

"You know how it is. And best of all, the face stuff is in this outfit. With the other I can just be myself."

Riding up in the self-service elevator at Jenson's hotel, Henderson felt a small prickle of nervousness at the base of his skull. If he had guessed correctly, Grogan would have tried to get Jenson to sell him out. Probably successfully. It was conceivable—he froze motionless with the thought—that Jenson had already sold him out. That the police would be waiting for him in this room. But not likely. Grogan wouldn't want him under arrest, and able to pull strings. Grogan would want him dead. That wouldn't come yet. Not in Jenson's own room. Henderson left the elevator and walked down the hall. The strings were all in his hands; he would pull them when he chose. At his knock, Jenson opened the door a few inches, then pulled it wide when he saw who it was. Henderson strode in confidently, but his eyes were wary until he made sure no one else was in the room.

"Well?" he demanded without preamble.

"Hell, boss," Jenson said. "Something slipped up out there."

Jenson's manner, while ill-at-ease, showed that he had attained the precarious balance with his habit at which he functioned best. He was not glassy-eyed and oblivious from too recent a shot, nor was he shaking with need of his next. He was as nearly normal as it was possible for him to be.

"Tell me about it," Henderson said.

"He's in with the cops out there," Jenson said. "They spotted us right off. They picked DeCarlo up, and followed him back to the motel." He shot an uneasy glance at Henderson. "At least, they must have. The cops didn't come in then, but Grogan followed DeCarlo. He wanted to talk to us."

"What did he have to say?"

"He just got tough. Said to tell you next time he would shoot on sight. I think he means it, too."

Henderson nodded, trying to appear worried. "Was that all he said?"

"Yeah. It all added up to that, anyhow."

The little man was having trouble concealing his nervousness. Henderson was almost amused at the transparency. This idiot was trying to outfox him.

"That the only time you saw him?" Henderson asked.

"Yeah. But boss, there was another funny thing."

"Spill it."

"After Grogan left, while we were just sitting around the joint, the cops came. They pulled DeCarlo in again, and took Small with him. They didn't want me. I can't figure it."

He was sweating profusely now. Henderson watched the little man with a close, sardonic scrutiny.

"Can't you really, Kicker?" he asked. "I can."

"What do you mean by that?"

"I mean I think you ought to tell me what Grogan wanted," Henderson said softly. "When he came back the second time. When he had you alone!"

"What the hell you talking about?"

"About Grogan's proposition. He came to see you again, didn't he?"

"Hell, no. I can't figure the whole thing. The boys say the coppers didn't want much out of them, either. Just sweated them awhile and let them go again. But I can't figure why they didn't take me."

Henderson stood up and smiled at the little man. He knew all he needed to know.

"Well, forget it," he said. "Grogan knows we can spot him, wherever he goes. That's really all I wanted done. You got along fine, Kicker."

Relief brightened the pinched features. "Thanks, boss. What you got for me now?"

"Just sit tight. If you get picked up here, you don't know a thing about me. You understand the routine."

"Sure, boss. Sure."

Outside in the hall, Henderson's face set with the determination of a course resolved. It was time for the wind-up. First the transfer of the money, then the finish of Charley Norris and Kicker Jonson. Things were working out just as he had planned.

CHAPTER 7

Grogan sat in the living room of the cabana, watching Betsy and Vic as they turned the pages of a picture book across the room. Rocco was beside the window. The last week had been peaceful; the days had come and gone with no alarm of any sort. And yet the tension had heightened with each hour. They were all on edge, jumpy. Grogan knew that Betsy was feeling it too.

"Why don't you two go get some air?" Grogan asked. "Betsy and I will have dinner sent in. Sort of a picnic, all by ourselves."

"I want Vic to stay," Betsy said.

Ordinarily she would have leaped at a chance to do anything alone with her father. She was just being contradictory. Grogan told himself it was because of the strain.

"Vic will stay, baby," Vic said soothingly. "You go, Steve. You've been sticking too close."

Grogan had no place to go. And wherever he went the same thing would be on his mind, nagging at him. Seven days. It was too long. He should have heard by now. If Jenson intended to play ball with him, there had been plenty of time. Grogan shook his head.

He saw Rocco stiffen and peer out the window.

"I'll be damned," Rocco said softly. "Not trouble," he added quickly at Grogan jumped to his feet. "Not shooting trouble, that is. It's the old man."

Grogan looked out in time to see the solid, middle-aged man turn off the sidewalk toward their door. He was wearing a gray business suit and a stiff felt hat,

making no concessions at all to the heat of the desert
sunshine. Inspector Julius Morrison might have just
stepped from behind his desk at headquarters.

Grogan opened the door. "Off your beat, aren't you,
officer?"

Morrison said: "Hello, Grogan." He didn't smile or
offer to shake hands.

Betsy was unaware of the constraint of the meeting.
Recognizing Morrison, she tumbled from Vic's lap and
ran to him, crowing with delight. "Uncle Julius," she
said. "You came to see me!"

The inspector did not resist the invitation of the up-
stretched arms. When he picked Betsy up, the smile
which lighted his severe, banker's face made him less
ominous. He even permitted the smile to rest on
Grogan for a moment.

"Of course I came to see my girl," he said. "How are
you honey?"

"Fine. What did you bring me?"

For a moment the Inspector was flustered. "I don't
have it with me," he said. "I left the present at the
hotel, but I'll get it." He put her down again and drew
a coin from his pocket. "Right now why don't you get
Rocco to take you over to the store to see what you
can buy with this?"

Rocco moved quickly, obviously glad of the excuse to
leave. Vic picked up her handbag and followed them
out the door. She threw Grogan one look, a desperate,
intent look which tried to tell him something. Then
Grogan was alone with Inspector Morrison.

"Drink?" Grogan asked.

"No, thanks. This isn't a social call, Grogan."

"I didn't figure it was."

Grogan could not put down a feeling of defiance,

which he knew to be childish, but he was not embarrassed. Damn it, he had done what he had to do. Morrison's judgment made no real difference.

The Inspector smiled again. "I didn't come to lecture, either. Don't think I'm blaming you, Steve. You've had a lot on your mind."

"How did you find me?" Grogan was concerned, now that the first surprise was over. This could be serious. "Did Bill Mallory . . ."

"Not Mallory. Another friend of yours sang me a song. Dandy Jim DeCarlo."

"I might have figured that. What did it buy him?"

"Nothing. Dandy Jim wasn't very healthy at the moment, and he's dead now. He just wanted to do a lot of talking before he died. I guess he thought a word from me might help with the judge on the other side."

Grogan kept his face inscrutable. Dandy Jim dead. That didn't sound as though anything were going according to plan.

"How did he get it?" he asked.

"A hand grenade. Messy. It was a miracle he lived long enough to talk at all." The Inspector was watching Grogan closely. "He couldn't tell us why. Or who. He was in his apartment, drinking with his pal Tony Small. Just the two of them. Jim passed out. When he came to, he was on the floor, crowded between a big overstuffed chair and the wall. There were voices in the room. Then an explosion. That's all he knows."

"Was Small killed?" Grogan, thinking furiously, could make no manner of sense out of all this.

"Blown to hell. At least three grenades were tossed in that room. Being on the floor and behind the chair gave DeCarlo what little protection he got."

"What about their sidekick, Jenson?" Grogan asked. "The three of them were out here together last week."

"No sign of him. The third body was Henderson."

Grogan sat very still. He felt that he waited an eternity, with those cold, expressionless eyes watching him, before the Inspector went on.

"Yes, we finally found Henderson. He took one of those grenades right in the face. No need to fret over your testimony now."

And there it was. Grogan, telling himself that he should feel only relief, was conscious instead of a dull sickness at the pit of his stomach he knew he would carry for the rest of his life. He had done what he thought he had to do, but the hundred thousand he had promised wasn't any part of the price he was going to have to pay.

"You come all the way out here to tell me that?" he asked.

"No." The Inspector's face was blank. "I thought there might be some things you could tell me."

"You expect me to cry because they got to Henderson?"

"Not cry, just talk. Who do you think I should look for, Steve? You know the mob better than anyone else. We wouldn't have uncovered Henderson at all if it hadn't been for you. Tell me some of the things I need to know."

So the old man had guessed. He couldn't be sure, of course, so long as Kicker Jenson was free and not talking, but from three thousand miles away his policeman's instinct had sized up the situation and led him straight to Grogan. It was a disquieting thought.

"You've got all I know on paper already," Grogan

said. "It's all in my reports. I don't have any idea who killed Henderson. It could have been any of them, figuring the heat would die down if he didn't come to trial."

The Inspector didn't dignify that with an answer. It didn't make sense, of course. Henderson, the quiet man, the almost unknown man, might have killed any of the gang to protect himself, but they were known anyway. Getting rid of Henderson couldn't help them at all.

"Why not let it alone?" Grogan asked. "The ring is smashed. Why keep picking at it?"

The Inspector's lips tightened. "Because I know you, Grogan. I know how your mind works. I know there's more behind this than a bunch of hoodlums falling out. First you ran out on me. I don't blame you too much for that, or at least I can understand it. Your kid was in danger, and better men than you, or me either for that matter, have let that break their nerve. But you want me to believe you just ran for this hole like a rabbit and didn't make a move to fight back. I can't buy that, Grogan."

"Hell, are you trying to pin this killing on me?" Grogan, knowing the charade to be pointless, still simulated elaborate surprise. "I haven't been out of town for two weeks. Bill Mallory can vouch for that."

"Sure he can. You didn't do it yourself, did you Grogan?"

The contempt flicked Grogan's ego, even though he recognized it as a deliberate attempt to get under his skin. He felt his face flush.

"I would have killed him if I could," he said. "And dragged the body down to city hall and bragged about it. You might have given me a medal. This way, one of his pals did it. What's the difference? Why not just be satisfied with the result?"

"You know why I can't be satisfied. I think you paid to have Henderson rubbed out. If it would end there, I might close my eyes to it. Probably would. But it won't end. These things always come out. Whoever your trigger man was—and Kicker Jenson is the one we are looking for—he will talk, he will spend his money and come back for more. That will give you a choice again. You can pay, or you can kill him. One thing will lead to another. I'm no happier about a killer cop running loose than I would be over any other kind of killer. That's the way I see it, Grogan."

Listening to the expressionless voice drone on, that was the way Grogan saw it too. He was in a box, a tight trap with no discernible exit and with walls that slowly closed in on him. He lit a cigarette and made himself grin at the Inspector.

"You seem to have made up your mind," he said, "so there is no point in my arguing with you. Are you expecting a confession?"

Inspector Morrison laughed. It was neither forced nor artificial, but contained genuine amusement. Grogan thought it held a hint of affection, or at least friendship, too.

"Look, Steve," Morrison said, "I'm not trying to nail you to the wall. I'm out here to keep you from doing that to yourself. We want you back on the team, with no hard feelings over the past. Like I said, I might have done the same thing myself."

"The way you just lined up a case against me, I'm interested to see how you figure to get me back on the side of the angels. Not that there is any truth to this pipedream, of course."

"This way." Morrison leaned forward, his eyes earnest and commanding. "I'm basing it all on the assumption there has been no payoff yet. Am I right?"

"Go ahead. This is your fairy tale."

"Okay. No payoff. I want you to give me the story, all of it. We'll pick up your trigger man. If he's taken alive, and that's no certainty, we can discount his talk by saying you were working with me all along. You can deny offering to pay him for killing Henderson, and say you were offering a bribe for information leading to Henderson's capture. How about it, Steve?"

That was the way life ran, Grogan thought wearily. Once you dropped the rules and began to play it freehand, you got in deeper and deeper. The Inspector was offering him a way out, one that would probably work. Most men would say he was asking nothing worse of him, nothing so bad, really, as Grogan had already done when he made the deal with Kicker Jenson. Nothing worse than he had done when he ran out on the department and tried to take Betsy away to safety.

To Grogan it was worse. He had given his word. He had said to Jenson: "And you'll be dealing with Steve Grogan. You know me, you've known about me for years. You know my word's good for the money. I was an honest cop when the money was all around me for the asking. Have you any doubts I'll pay off?" Now Morrison was asking him to cross Jenson, turn him in and rat on him, just on the assumption that Jenson would try a double-cross. He probably would try, but he hadn't yet. The other things Grogan had done involved no personal betrayal. In running away he had been ducking out on his duty to an impersonal society. When he made the deal for killing Henderson

he had been after a declared enemy. This action
Morrison was suggesting would be turning on a man
who, even though a criminal, still trusted Grogan. He
couldn't do it.

"Well, Steve?" Morrison showed no impatience.

"Well what? This is your dream, you know, not mine.
There isn't a word of truth in it. Henderson's death
can't touch me."

The Inspector rose slowly to his feet. "No use talking
about it, eh, Grogan?" His voice was sad.

"Nothing to talk about."

"Then God help you, Grogan. I'm going to get you. I
have to do it."

Watching the gray man go down the walk, Grogan
felt no animosity toward him. According to Morrison's
code, which so recently had been Grogan's own, there
was no choice. He had to do it, if he could.

CHAPTER 8

By the time Vic and Rocco brought Betsy back,
Grogan had made up his mind. For good or bad, he
had made his throw. Perhaps Jenson wouldn't be
picked up. Perhaps if he was he wouldn't talk, after
all, squealing on Grogan would be strapping himself
in the chair. When he came back for his money, Grogan
would pay him off. He had been holding the cash, in a
briefcase in the back room, for three days. It could be
traced to him, of course, but proving that he gave it to
Jenson would be tough. He could always say he had
lost it gambling. He would start hitting the spots
immediately. If Jenson tried to play leech later on . . .
well, he would cross that bridge when he came to it.

"We've lost a friend," he told Vic and Rocco. "The Inspector was telling me about Mr. Henderson's fatal accident."

Vic started to speak, glanced down at Betsy, and was quiet. Rocco's dark face gleamed with satisfaction.

"Hallelujah," Rocco said. "That about winds it up, doesn't it, Steve?"

Grogan nodded. He was troubled to see Vic pick Betsy up abruptly and walk to the back bedroom with her, refusing to look at either of them. Vic's tight features showed she was about to cry.

Rocco shrugged. "Women," he said. "They look at things a little different sometimes."

"Yeah."

"Vic is upset about Betsy. Her future." Rocco was embarrassed, but determined to see it through. "We've been talking it over, Steve. When this is all finished, we're going to have to split up. Our setup won't work out forever."

"Time enough to decide that."

"Sure. I just want you to know we understand. Vic and Betsy, they're getting too attached to each other. You'll want the kid to grow up to be, well, hell, a lady, like her mother. We don't fit in." He put up a hand to silence Grogan's attempted speech. "Vic will never marry me. Even if that little bitch Rosa would give me a divorce, the church means more to Vic than it does to me." Rocco's grin was twisted. "What sense can you expect out of a Swede Catholic? She'll sleep with me, but it would be a sin to marry me. I'm dumb, but even I know better than that."

"Marriage is something permanent," Grogan said. "The other, I suppose she is always telling herself, is a temporary mistake she'll break off sooner or later."

"I'm afraid it's going to be sooner. She's going to church all the time now, Steve. Whenever she gets a free minute. We're going to split up. And she won't stay with Betsy, either. Right or wrong, she's made up her dumb Swede mind the kid will be better off without her. She's doing it because she loves Betsy, Steve."

"I know. I won't ever be able to repay you and Vic for what you've done for me, Rocco. We'll have to hold steady a little while yet, though. The old man thinks I had Henderson rubbed out."

Grogan told him about the Inspector's visit, in word-for-word detail. Rocco listened intently, his dark face impassive, his only movement the drumming of his fingers on the arm of his chair. When Grogan finished Rocco laughed.

"Sticky," he said, "but it was the best way out. Was Jenson the man, Steve?"

"You don't need to know stuff like that."

"Oh, yes, I do. Jenson is our one danger now, and I'm just the boy to take care of that. Leave him to me, Steve."

Grogan said shortly that he wanted Jenson left alone. Rocco's attitude made him see, more clearly than ever, the essential rightness of Inspector Morrison's position. He and Rocco couldn't go on like a pair of jungle animals, killing whatever stepped in their paths. Jenson probably had friends in it with him. One thing would lead to another. What security was there for Betsy in that?

Grogan sat at his usual table at the far end of the bar, listening to Terry run through a number. The place was quiet until the small, sultry voice died away;

then it broke into the usual bedlam. Terry smiled in his direction and began to pick her way through the crowd toward him.

The three men in the orchestra stood up and stretched. Grogan knew them all casually through Terry. Pop, the leader, was incongruous in the setting. He was a big man, middle-aged, almost bald and running a bit to fat. He looked thoroughly respectable, more like a prosperous businessman who perhaps taught Sunday school than a saxophone player in a second-rate desert joint. His manner toward Terry was paternally protective, and he had a hard suspicious eye for Grogan.

"Another night," Terry said, sliding into the booth beside Grogan. "You look tired, Steve."

"Aren't we all?" Grogan was filled with a vast distaste for the surroundings. "How long are you going to stick with this sort of thing?"

"As long as I have to eat, I guess. Music can be a tough racket, when you don't quite have what it takes. I'm lucky Pop has been a friend of the family for years, so he took me on when I decided to try the desert for a while." She put her hand over his. "I didn't know I would find you here, too."

Grogan was disturbed by the warmth of her fingers. It was no part of his plan to permit himself to feel so strongly for any girl.

He said: "You shouldn't have to sing here. You're head and shoulders above the rest of this crowd."

"Not head and shoulders, just chest and legs." She squeezed his hand. "You're a good guy, Grogan, and a friend of mine, but you have a tin ear in more ways than one. Pop has the talent in this troupe. Any big band would be glad to have him. He has a wife and three children, though, and doesn't want to travel. He'll be up early in the morning giving music lessons to a band of young hopefuls."

Grogan didn't want to talk about Pop or the band. Most of all he did not want to think about the fact that Terry had arrived at the Casa Carillon shortly after he and Betsy checked in. It was a nagging, disloyal thought he could not quite hold in check. The music started again, a sensuous tango.

"Dance with me, Steve?" Terry asked. "You never have danced with me."

She felt small and fragile in his arms. She was an excellent dancer, following his purposefully intricate moves without effort. When the music stopped she looked up at him in surprise.

"You never cease to amaze me, Grogan," she said. "Were you a professional gigolo in an earlier life? I've never known a better dancer."

"Police training," Grogan said modestly. "I was assigned to a case at a dance studio once. I had to go through the whole course three times before they pulled me off it. I never broke the case, but I learned to do a mean rhumba."

Terry cuddled beside him again in the booth. "You're almost a handsome man when you aren't scowling, Grogan. Not too collar-ad. Maybe the tin ear saves you from that."

"It is not a . . ."

"All right, all right. Don't be so sensitive."

Grogan knew she expected him to kiss her. And he wanted to—wanted it more than he had wanted anything in a long, long time. But this was no time for him to get entangled in anything approaching sentiment, and so he shifted slightly on the hard bench, moving away from her.

"Don't look so worried," Terry said. "I'm not trying to compromise you."

"Damn it, don't talk like that."

"Like what?" She smiled at him. "Steve, why can't you relax more with me? I know none of this is permanent. But for now, why can't we just be ourselves—be friends?"

Grogan avoided her eyes.

"If it isn't permanent," he said carefully, "then it isn't going to be at all. Pop is signaling for you now."

While Terry went through her number, Grogan got up and strolled to the bar. He was staring moodily into his glass when a hand touched his elbow.

"Well, neighbor."

Grogan looked up to find himself seated beside Liza Carrol, the blond occupant of the cabana next to his. Vic's candidate, he remembered awkwardly, for the next Mrs. Grogan. He tried to return the casual friendliness of her smile.

The girl—or woman, she was approaching thirty— was certainly pleasant to look at. Long yellow hair curled simply back from the perfect oval of her face. There was a calm, aloof quality to her beauty but her quick smile suggested a warmth underneath. Her severely tailored silk suit set her apart from the motley crowd. Grogan remembered her in other costumes— in Bermuda shorts in front of her cabin, in a bathing suit at the pool—and knew the perfect figure she was now making no effort to display.

"I haven't seen you in here before," Grogan said.

She shrugged. "I don't care to be a lone woman in bars. Now that my father is here . . . I don't believe you met my father when he got in this afternoon. He was quite captivated by Betsy."

The bald, middle-aged man in a white linen suit and rimless glasses seated on the other side of Liza reached a hand across to Grogan. "John Bragg," he said. His handshake was loose, the palm clammy. He said pleasantly that he had been wanting to meet Betsy's father.

"Dad hasn't been well," Liza said. "I've been urging him to come out here for a rest. He shouldn't be up tonight, but he insists on seeing the bright lights. I suspect he thought I was restless."

"The strain is more than I expected," Mr. Bragg admitted. "Perhaps we should be going back soon."

It followed naturally enough that Grogan should invite Liza to remain out with him, and she seemed pleased to accept. Terry was watching from the bandstand and Grogan felt a distinct unease, but there was no help for it. Then Liza looked doubtfully at her father.

"You're sure you won't need me, dad?"

"I can still put myself to bed. Entertaining you is the problem I would prefer to leave to a younger man."

When he had gone, Liza flashed her warm smile at Grogan. "This is an exciting town. Doesn't it do something to you?"

"It hasn't until now," Grogan said. He was startled at himself. "Ready for another drink?"

Liza danced well, although not with Terry's almost professional skill. She took Grogan's excellence for granted, without comment. She was taller than Terry; her head could not have rested comfortably on his shoulder even had she been so inclined. Grogan was irritated with himself for the comparison. This was no time for even one woman to be on his mind, much less two. And Terry's attitude bothered him. Without making a point of it she contrived never to meet his eye, never to be standing at a point where he could conveniently speak to her without being obvious about abandoning Liza.

Liza drank sparingly, but the liquor put a sparkle in her eye which had not been there before. Grogan could not tell whether it was his imagination or not that she melted just a bit more into his arms as they danced. It was pleasant in itself but embarrassing because of Terry's silent presence. He was relieved when Liza glanced at her watch.

"I must be getting back. I have to see whether dad has settled down for the night."

As they strolled across the grass she walked close to him, without touching him.

"Steve," she said gently, "you aren't a happy man, are you?"

"What?" He was startled.

"And you should be, you know."

"Should I?" He knew that it came out bitterly.

"Yes, you should. Betsy. Whatever else happened, whatever you lost, you have that. Try to look at it that way. It would have made all the difference to me if . . ."

It wasn't a thing you could go around explaining to people. Grogan had told Terry his troubles because the situation demanded it, but there was no necessity for that now. He was annoyed, knowing that there was no justice to his feeling. Still, any insinuation that he held Betsy lightly was enough to send his temper flaring. She must have sensed his disapproval.

"I'm sorry," she said, her voice small. "I shouldn't have said that, should I?"

"Don't be sorry. It is true, and perhaps I need reminding once in a while. You're right, of course. I have business troubles on my mind. It isn't unhappiness."

At the door Liza turned toward him. "Thanks, Steve. It's been a lovely evening." Her voice was soft.

Grogan had not intended to kiss her, and was surprised with himself when he did so. After the first hesitation she returned the pressure of his lips without constraint. It was pleasant, but without any of the excitement Terry aroused in him.

When Liza went inside Grogan hesitated a moment, looking at the darkened windows of his cabana and then at the lights coming from the bar back at the highway. The music came faintly to him. At length he turned and retraced his steps toward the music.

Terry was sitting in her usual chair on the bandstand when he came in. She did not see Grogan until he touched her arm.

"How about a glass of champagne?" he asked.

Her pale face was unsmiling. "Thanks, Steve. I don't feel up to it tonight." Her attention did not stay with him; she turned and signaled her appreciation to Pop for the chorus he had just finished.

Bewildered and a little hurt, Grogan walked back to his usual booth. He didn't want to stay now, but he could scarcely turn around and leave the moment he came in. The bartender brought him a beer without his ordering. He grinned at Grogan, started to speak, then checked himself and left without a word. Grogan grunted. He was everybody's pal tonight but Terry's. The thought bothered him.

Terry sang again. Another torch song, a sad song, which had the usual effect on Grogan. She might not have real talent, as she said, but she sent shivers up and down his spine. Grogan wondered why his dancing with Liza had put him on her black book so completely. Her failure to look his way with the usual smile was quite pointed. Of course, she would be very tired. It was after three o'clock, the normal closing time, but tonight the crowd was better than usual and the management was no doubt nursing out a few extra nickels. The thought made Grogan indignant.

Pop left the stand and walked the length of the room toward Grogan. He sat down heavily on the bench across from Grogan, sighing deeply as he leaned back and relaxed.

Grogan signaled the bartender. "What will you have, Pop?"

Pop waved the bartender back. "Nothing for me. I have to drink enough of that slop when the customers send one up for the band. Big time operators!"

He was being more vehement than usual. Pop seldom let himself become stirred up. Grogan wondered what he wanted; the musician had never sought him out before. They sat in silence while Terry finished her chorus and bowed in acknowledgment of the applause.

"A good kid," Pop said.

"Sure."

"Not a tramp. Not the kind you usually meet in this business. She talks tough because she has seen too many movies and thinks it is the thing to do, but not a tramp. I've known her family all her life."

"Are you warning me, Pop?" Grogan was amused.

There was no answering smile. Grogan realized that this big, respectable looking man might actually be very tough indeed if he had to be. He was not in the least threatening, but he sat there big and solid while he spoke his piece and he looked ready to back it up in any way necessary. Grogan revised his earlier opinion of Pop just a bit.

"Not a warning," Pop said. "I don't figure that's necessary with you. I just want to remind you Terry is a good girl, not used to being mixed up in any shady deals. She isn't going to be while she stays with my band."

Grogan sighed. "She isn't going to be mixed up in anything on my account, Pop. I agree, she's a fine girl. I wouldn't do anything to hurt her."

"Sometimes a man doesn't mean everything that happens." Pop remained uncompromising. "You really are an ex-cop?"

"Yeah."

"All right, Grogan. Sorry if I stuck my nose in where it doesn't belong. Well, I guess it's about time for me to go back up and sign off for the night. The union would be on me now if it knew we were still kicking."

Pop got to his feet, rolling mournful eyes at Grogan. "No hard feelings, Steve?"

"None at all."

"Then maybe you won't mind just one more tip from the old man. When you come to see a girl, Steve, especially a girl who has been thinking about you all night, it isn't a bad idea to wipe off the lipstick from your last port of call. It makes for better feeling all around."

He left Grogan scrubbing furiously at his lips with his handkerchief.

CHAPTER 9

As Grogan went out the front door of the bar he hesitated under the neon sign, taking his usual quick look around for trouble. A rented car was parked at the curb, its occupant leaning out the window.

"Lieutenant," the man in the car said.

Grogan walked over to the sedan. The street was brightly lit, there was no one in the car but the driver. He kept his hands negligently in sight on the door.

"Yeah?" Grogan said.

Grogan could read nothing from the face looking out at him. It was a pale face, one that had not been long in this climate. About twenty-five. Clothes which cost real money. Not a policeman. Nothing about him to mark the mobster, either, except the too-quiet, ice blue eyes.

"I don't know you," Grogan said.

"You can call me Smitty. We have a mutual friend."

"Get to it."

"My friend's name is Jenson. He says you have a package for him. I'm to deliver it to him. Right now isn't a good time for him to be traveling."

It had to come, of course. This or something like it. Grogan was not surprised.

"I've got nothing for Jenson," he said. "If I did have, I would want a little better identification."

Smitty shrugged. "I see your point, lieutenant, but what the hell? You don't expect Kicker to walk up in person, do you?"

"Can't he use a telephone?"

Their eyes clashed, and Smitty shrugged again, an

indication of withdrawal. "All right. You'll get a ring in a couple of hours. I'm glad you're playing this straight, lieutenant."

The words were light, unaccented, but there was menace in them. Grogan felt a weariness deep in his bones. This was the sort of thing which might follow him forever.

"I'll be straight," he said, "to the exact extent of the deal. No more, no less. You boys want to keep that damned well in mind. I bought what I wanted and I'll pay for it, but don't get the idea you can shake me down. Understand?"

"Sure, lieutenant, sure. Kicker will call you, and you'll get word tomorrow where you can hand over the package."

"Not tomorrow," Grogan said. "And not in the open like this, either. This was stupid. Don't do it again."

"You looking for trouble?"

"Of course I'm looking for trouble. I'll pay, but I want some precaution taken. I don't feel safe having you take the money out of town, now that you and I have been seen together. You couldn't explain where you got a roll that size without dragging me in. The New York police are suspicious of me, and might have a tail on me. I want to take a couple of days hitting the gambling spots, so I can have a story on what I did with the money if it is traced out of my account."

"I don't like to hang around . . ."

"Take it or leave it," Grogan said flatly.

"All right. I'll get in touch in two days."

Smitty started the car and drove away.

The phone call came through in less than two hours. Grogan picked up the receiver and said "hello" in a tone which came out louder than he expected.

For a moment he heard only the humming of the wire; there was a bad connection somewhere along the line. Then a voice, faint and husky, familiar, but not definitely recognizable.

"Good vacation, lieutenant?" the voice said.

"Good enough."

"Just wanted to tell you to be nice to my friend Smitty, lieutenant. Treat him like you would me."

"I don't like this," Grogan said.

"But you'll play ball. Like you told me, your word is good. I've counted on that. Counted a hell of a lot on it."

"All right." Grogan made up his mind that he was talking to Jenson. Either to him or to someone Jenson had told the whole story, and Kicker would not be apt to do that. Hell, he couldn't ask for fingerprints. "I'll do business," Grogan said. "In a couple of days." He hung up the receiver.

Grogan sat talking with Bill Mallory the next morning in the Chief's office. Mallory was preoccupied, a worried frown knotting his forehead, but his handclasp had been as warm as ever.

Grogan knew well enough what the trouble was. Inspector Morrison had been in and talked to Mallory. It put the Chief in a tough spot. Between him and Grogan was a bond stretching back through the years, back to the time Grogan was a rookie and Mallory, a veteran policeman on the New York force, was in real trouble. He had been charged with extortion and blackmail, and the department, in the throes of a publicity-heated cleanup, was ready to throw Mallory to the wolves. Grogan, working on his first big case, let his obstinacy and his faith in Mallory break through the prejudices of the top brass and cleared Mallory. Mallory hadn't forgotten it and never would.

"Morrison been in to see you?" Grogan asked.

"That's right."

"Don't let it bother you, Bill. Do what he asks. Cooperate with him."

"Hell, Grogan, he wants . . ."

"I know what he wants. He asked you to put a tail on me, watch my contacts, tie me up with the payoff on Henderson's killing in New York. You'll have to go along, Bill. If you don't, he'll put men of his own in. You can't afford to be on the wrong side when this breaks."

"I won't sell you out, either, Steve. I'd have done the same thing in your shoes."

"Maybe. Maybe Morrison is just imagining what I did. Go along with him. You can't hurt me. I asked you for protection from mobsters, and you've given it to me all the way. That's all I needed. Morrison hasn't a thing on me and he can't get anything. You do just what he asks."

Watching the relief take possession of Mallory, Grogan wished that he could have the inner confidence his words had implied. He had convinced Bill. Convincing himself was something else again. Grogan knew he was going to have to play this very carefully.

"How about up till now, Bill? Did you have a man on me last night?"

The relief left Mallory's face as he looked thoughtfully at Grogan. He said at length: "No."

"Did Morrison?"

Another long pause. "To the best of my knowledge, he did not. I can't be sure. We didn't part on the best of terms."

"Well, patch it up with him. Last night doesn't make any difference anyway. I was just curious."

When Grogan returned to the cabana, he found something approaching a party in progress. Vic was serving tea to Liza Carrol and Terry. He was relieved to see that apparently Terry was no longer angry. She gave him a quick, gamin grin as he entered the room. Liza smiled pleasantly while Grogan picked Betsy up and hugged her tightly.

Watching Vic with the tea utensils, Grogan was struck by the disloyal thought that she looked just what she was, an ex-carnival girl trying to be a lady. Rocco, dark and enigmatic in the background, pointed up the picture. Betsy, on her good behavior, fluttered about being a hostess. Grogan wandered out on the porch and stood lost in thought until Terry joined him.

Terry, looking up at him, struck him as being very young, and very lovely. Her dark beauty was in its way as striking as Liza's more polished blond elegance. Terry wore a long-sleeved blue dress. The tan on her legs must have come from a lotion bottle.

"Mad at me, Grogan?" she asked.

He shook his head. "Should I be?"

"I'm not mad at you anymore. I decided I was taking life too seriously. Besides, I got even. I let Rollie kiss me once or twice when he walked me home." Rollie was one of the boys in the band.

Grogan could think of no suitable comment. Terry continued to smile at him.

"Was it fun, Grogan, kissing the blond goddess? The ladylike goddess?"

"Stop that."

"Don't be too taken in by that finishing school

accent." Mischief crinkled the corners of her eyes. "If that's what you want, just remember I can talk that way too when I put my mind to it."

Startled, Grogan realized that from her first words on the porch Terry's voice had carried neither the sultry allure of her stage manner nor the flatness she always seemed to turn to as a contrast when she left the bandstand. It was clear, soft, and plainly enunciated. As a matter of fact, not unlike Liza Carrol's.

"We better get back to the party," Grogan said.

Vic greeted them with a faint frown. Grogan was aware of a subtle difference between her manner toward Terry and toward Liza. Liza was Vic's candidate for a post that wasn't even open, Grogan thought bitterly.

The telephone jangled through the buzz of conversation. Grogan picked up the receiver to hear Mallory's voice. "Is the baby all right?" Mallory asked.

Grogan's world exploded around him. The small talk in the room stilled immediately at his expression.

"Yes. Why shouldn't she be?"

"I just got a call from Morrison. He had some information he thought you might need. He wants to stay on your side, Steve, as much as he can."

"Sure, sure. What was the word?"

"They were dragging the river, on another matter altogether. They picked up a body with a concrete footwork. Kicker Jenson."

Grogan felt as if he had been hit in the stomach. He had been so sure—so almost sure, anyway—about the voice on the telephone.

"How long had he been dead?" he asked.

"Quite a while. Nearly a week, they think."

"Identification positive?"

"Positive. The face wasn't much, but they were able to get prints. Morrison says there is no room for doubt."

Grogan took a moment to absorb it. A week. Soon after Jenson talked to Grogan for the last time. It might mean . . . hell, it might mean anything.

"Now, Steve," Mallory said, "you're back with us. I think you better stay there. Have you been contacted about a payoff?"

Grogan's mind was racing. He had no intention of telling too much, he meant to get his hands on Smitty, and squeeze the information he wanted out of him. He could do that better if he wasn't hampered by any police department.

"I'll call you back later," he said.

He was so preoccupied when he hung up the receiver he hardly noticed the party melting away.

CHAPTER 10

The afternoon and evening stretched out endlessly for Grogan. There was none of the exhilaration of combat in the situation. It was just a dirty, messy business, a shakedown from someone who knew of his pact with Jenson. However it went it probably would not be the last. It was the sort of thing he would have to expect from now on.

By nine o'clock, Betsy in bed, Grogan, Vic and Rocco sat quietly in the living room. Only Vic, white-faced and tight-lipped, showed the emotional strain. Once she tried to argue.

"Give it up, Steve," she said. "Please. Catch the morning plane to New York. Let Inspector Morrison handle everything."

"I can't. If I miss contact here, they'll have the jump on me. I won't know where, or who, or when. I just know someone will be around, someday. At least this way I can get my hands on Smitty and make him talk. I want to know what is going on."

At ten the phone rang. Grogan, sitting just beside it, had the receiver in his hand before the first tinkle had stopped. "Grogan," he said.

"Hello, lieutenant. Smitty."

"I told you not for two days," Grogan said, hiding his elation at the call.

"Things have changed. I need to see you tonight. Have you got the money?"

Caution made Grogan say: "Not tonight. Not yet. I don't want to talk over the phone. Where are you?"

"Are you trying to cross me, lieutenant?"

"I told you I would pay for what I bought. But I want to talk first."

The phone hummed in Grogan's ear. He began to fear Smitty had gone away, and then the answer came. Calmly, with no trace of irritation.

"All right. Come down to the bus depot, lieutenant. Wait there for me. I want some bright lights around."

The receiver clicked. Grogan told Vic and Rocco how the conversation had gone. Vic clutched at his hand.

"Don't go, Steve. It's a trap. At least, don't go alone."

"That's silly. The guy is scared of me. Besides, I'm in no danger until after the payoff, and he knows I don't have the money with me. Betsy, maybe." Just saying it sent the familiar chill, through Grogan. "They might try to get her, to turn the screws tighter on me. I want Rocco here with you and Betsy, and I don't intend to let the police in on this."

Still Vic kept her grip on his hand. "Take Rocco with you, and we can ask one of the policemen to stay with us. Please, Steve."

"Might be a good idea," Rocco said.

"No. Smitty would know Rocco, just as he knew me. He won't even come near me if I'm not alone. I've got to go, Vic. Once I get my hands on Smitty, the bright lights won't help him much."

They finally let him go. Rather, he terminated the conversation by putting on his coat and leaving, while Vic started to cry and Rocco watched with his usual frozen-faced calm. For all his other concern, Grogan found time to wonder again just how Rocco felt about Vic's attitude toward Grogan.

Grogan drove to town. He swung the Olds by the bus station, with its flood-lighted parking lot, and continued two blocks beyond to a side street. If he got a chance to march Smitty out of there, as he intended to do, he didn't want to wrestle him into the car with a lot of people around. After parking he stood back away from the car, in the shadows of the mouth of an alley, while he surveyed the street. So far as he could tell he had not been followed from the Casa Carillon and he was not being observed now.

The bus station was indeed brightly lit, and almost empty. A few patrons dozed on the benches. The girl at the magazine counter yawned behind her hand. The ticket desk was deserted. Grogan stood in the doorway, looking over the room, and felt cheated. There was no sign of Smitty.

A newsboy, in his early teens, crossed the lobby. "Are you Mr. Grogan?" he asked.

"That's right."

"I've got a note for you." The boy fished in his pocket

and produced a scrap of paper. "A guy told me to give it to you."

Grogan read the note. It said: "I'll meet you in my room at the Congo Hotel. 205. Come alone, and don't use the phone first."

Grogan felt for a dollar and handed it to the boy. "Who gave you this, son?"

"Just a guy. I never saw him before."

"How did you recognize me?"

"He said you would be in in about ten minutes, waiting around for somebody. He said you would be a big, tough-looking character."

Grogan returned to his car. Still nobody on his trail, at least not close enough to spot. And except for the newsboy he had aroused no particular interest in the bus station. Nevertheless, he didn't like it. Smitty was being very cautious for a man who had approached him so openly before. Yet Grogan considered his reasoning as sound as it had been earlier. He would not be in any personal danger from Smitty until the money was in sight.

The Congo Hotel, the address of which Grogan looked up in a telephone booth at a service station, was in the skid row section. He parked almost directly in front of the hotel. He had never been here before, but he felt at home. Around here he would know what to expect.

The Congo was three stories high; two tiers of rooms over a ground floor pool hall. The neon sign was missing a couple of letters. A bum lounging in the door of the pool hall watched Grogan incuriously as he started up the stairs.

Halfway up he pulled his .38 from its belt holster and put it into the right-hand pocket of his coat, where he kept his fingers closed around the butt. If trouble came, nothing was faster than that. He paused at the head of the stairs, looking the lobby over.

The lobby was only a battered counter, a few frayed easy chairs, and a stack of magazines on a table. The still air, sour with the unwashed, old-cooking smell of all cheap hotels, was still muggy from the heat of the day.

Two men, transient laborers from the looks of their clothing, were talking to the clerk at the counter. And Smitty was sitting in one of the battered chairs, reading a newspaper. He looked up and nodded to Grogan.

As Grogan entered the lobby the laborers turned from the desk and started toward the stairway. They parted as they neared Grogan, and he realized that they meant to pass him on either side. He stepped quickly toward the wall, not really suspicious, but instinct warned him not to be surrounded. With his first movement he saw excitement break through the stolid mask of the nearer man, and he knew he was in trouble. He had time for the streaking thought: "I've made a mistake," and then they were both jumping for him, blackjacks swinging. He was aware of Smitty leaving his chair with a diving rush.

Grogan shot through his pocket at the first man, the one facing him. At the same moment he lashed out behind him with a foot and his left arm, and dropped to the floor to avoid the other blackjack. He lit solidly on his side, feeling the man behind him stumble over his legs as he went down. On the floor, the gun in his pocket was no use; he was rolling over and pulling it free when his head exploded.

CHAPTER 11

Henderson had spent a restless morning. He sat in the darkened living room, stripped to his shorts, and fretted over the decision which had dragged him out here to the edge of nowhere to see the job finished. It might prove to be a fatal move—he knew that. Certainly it was a far cry from his plan of disappearing back into his true identity with the fortune "Henderson" had accumulated. Thought of how close he had come to success set his nerves pulsing with fury.

Damn Charley Norris. That slippery little nonentity, the stupid tool who hadn't even been able to save his own life, had still managed with his last act to double-cross Henderson. He had died in Henderson's place as Henderson had intended, but toward the end he must have smelled a rat. The money, which Henderson thought had been safely transferred with the bulky corporation documents Norris gave him to sign, was out of reach without a further clearance from Norris, who was dead, damn him.

And so, Henderson told himself, he had no choice. From being a rich man he was down to a few paltry thousand, and the hundred grand Grogan had promised for the payoff was all-important to him. Grogan was the sort of fool who would pay on schedule, as long as he did not suspect what had happened. Then Henderson could fade away, not rich, but a long way from broke. Yes, he had to go through with this.

But perhaps he should not have come himself. It might have been better to leave it to Smitty and the girl. As for Grogan, he was unimportant. Let him show up with his testimony and his ledger with its names and dates. Henderson was through with the syndicate anyway, whether or not Grogan talked. If the gang once realized he was alive, and that he had engineered the wholesale killing of Norris and the rest, they would be out to get him. He had seen it happen before. Henderson had to stay dead, to Grogan, to the gang, to the world.

He briefly debated leaving town again, and knew he could not do it. The girl might be loyal, but Smitty would have to be held in line. She wouldn't be able to handle the situation if things got rough. She was too gentle, too . . .

Thought of her sent him pacing the room again. She had been gone too long, and it worried him. There was always the chance she would run out. Or . . . go over to Grogan. He was relieved when the front door opened to show him her pinched, frightened face.

"Time you were getting back," he told her.

"Marc, something has happened. He got a phone call. I'm sure he knows."

Henderson's nerves jumped. "Shut up!" he said, immediately aware that it was too loud. Any passerby could have heard him. He lowered his voice. "Don't get hysterical. Tell me what happened. Slow and easy, now."

She stood bolt upright in the middle of the room, fighting for calm. Her eyes were enormous. Henderson wondered that he could notice that; he had never paid much attention to her eyes before.

"Grogan got a phone call," she said. "Just a few minutes ago. Until then he had been relaxed and friendly. I'm sure nothing was worrying him. But after the call . . . I could tell from his end of the conversation that they have found Jenson's body. Marc, will he guess it all?"

Henderson watched her terror and knew he must not let his own dismay show. Grogan, of course, would eventually guess. He was a cop, and he had the time and money to press his inquiries. He would track down Smitty. He would find out how and when Jenson was killed. Then he would know Jenson had died before the supposed killing of Henderson, and from then on he would make tracking Henderson down his life's work.

Henderson's mind was made up. Grogan would have to go, and this proved how wise he had been to take the risk of coming here himself. He was on the spot, able to make the decisions. He would finish the job, through Smitty, and be on his way. No money, but he had started from scratch once before.

"Marc," she said, "you should have seen Grogan's face when he hung up the phone. That man is dangerous."

"Of course he's dangerous," he said. "Why do you think we're going to all this trouble?"

"I don't know. I'm just sure you're talking too big a risk, being here like this. What if he recognizes you?"

"In this outfit?" Henderson made himself laugh. "Don't worry your little head about that. Nobody in the world even suspects I'm within three thousand miles of here. Except you."

His apparent confidence had its effect. She collapsed in a chair and kicked off her shoes. Henderson thought she still contrived to look cool and immaculate. And . . . hell, ladylike. He enjoyed having her around. He would be sorry when . . .

"Won't it ever end, Marc?" she asked. "Why don't we forget Grogan, and leave? Go to South America or Mexico, as you promised."

"Not until I settle Grogan," he said impatiently.

It wouldn't do to let her know about the money. She would realize then, trusting though she had been, that he couldn't afford to take her with him. And that he couldn't afford to leave her behind knowing his appearance, either.

Henderson walked to the sink and poured himself a drink from the bottle on the drainboard. He wished he actually were as relaxed as he was trying to sound, but just going through the motions made him feel better. He was still the man in the driver's seat, after all. The drink bolstered him further, and made him almost satisfied with the plan evolving in his mind. On impulse, he walked back to the girl and put out a hand to grasp her wrist with a grip he knew would be painful.

"If you do as I say," he said, "we'll he okay."

"I will. Marc, you're hurting me."

Henderson didn't quite like the way she looked at him then. Something of the wary caution with which Charley Norris had regarded him, right at the last, showed in her eyes. He had to be careful. The suspicion hadn't helped Charley, in the long run, but it had ruined Henderson.

She was still necessary to him. He released her wrist and put an arm around her shoulders; her muscles were stiffly resistant under his touch. Henderson made his voice soft.

"Sorry if I sounded tough, baby. It's just that this is important, and you are the only one I can trust."

Still she did not relax. "I'm scared, Marc. It's Grogan. I don't believe we can go on fooling him forever."

"We won't even try." He squeezed her shoulder. "The time has come to get rid of Grogan, baby."

She pulled away. "Marc, isn't there any other way? Besides killing him? You said . . ."

Henderson smothered his irritation. This was no time to belt her one, to let the throbbing anger he was feeling take possession of him. When he had had nothing to fear from her, before she had this hold of being the only living person to know his present identity, he had been able to treat her roughly. Now it had to be easy and gentle. For a while.

"There isn't any other way, is there?" he asked. His tone was reasonable. "Not if they've found Jenson, and are suspicious. If you and I are going to be able to get away for a clean start, and live respectable, we can't have Grogan nosing around on the back trail. Can we?"

She sank into a chair and put her head in her hands. "Can we?" he asked again. "Be sensible."

She lifted her head to look at him. Her eyes were tortured, but he was relieved to see she could not hold his glance for more than a few seconds. She was having her qualms of conscience, but she wasn't ready to stand up to him yet. She would still do as he said.

"I don't want to be a part of it," she said.

"You never used to be so squeamish."

"You never used me for your finger man before. I just heard about things, or half knew them. This is different. I've met the man, played with his little girl. I guess I don't mind so much about him, but the child . . . Marc, I simply can't let anything happen to her."

Henderson pretended to consider. It made no real difference to him; the child's usefulness was in the past anyway. And it was important for her to think he was giving in to her. He knew it wouldn't do to change too easily; she would never swallow that. He made his voice rough again.

"You falling for that cop?" he asked. "Is that it? It's going to be him instead of me?"

"You know better, Marc. I said I didn't mind so much about him. But I won't let you harm the little girl. Please, Marc."

Henderson had difficulty hiding his glee. The jealousy pitch. That had been exactly the right touch. It turned her mind from dangerous channels. He shook his head in pretended exasperation.

"All right," he said, "if you won't, you won't. The kid is out. We'll work on something else. I won't let anything come between us, baby. You know that."

Apparently she bought it. She stood up again, her eyes sparkling.

"You won't be sorry, Marc. I promise you."

Henderson put his arms around her, finding her yielding and responsive this time. For a moment the passion she always aroused in him had the upper hand, but he caught himself. There was too much to do, too much at stake. He couldn't be fooling around with that now. He stepped back. "You always could drive me nuts, baby," he said, and the hoarseness of his voice was not entirely simulated. "Just stay away from that cop, that's all."

"All right, Marc. But I don't want to know anything about it."

Henderson crossed to the sofa and sat beside her, his hands moving soothingly over her shoulders. The anger he felt at any opposition was twitching his nerves, but he forced it under control.

"There is just one thing you will have to do, baby,"

he said. "So it will be clean. So they will believe it was an accident."

"No, Marc. Not me."

"Just one little thing," he said. "I'm going to have Smitty take him alive. Oh, he'll be knocked out, so he won't know what is going on. Smitty will drive him up into the mountains in his own car, and run it off a cliff. Just a routine accident."

She shook her head, eyes dilated with horror.

"I can't even bear to think about it," she said. "And if you must do it, why should I be connected?"

"Because without you, it's too old a gag. The oldest in the books. He would have no reason to be in the mountains, no reason to be driving alone. They wouldn't buy it. But it would be natural for him to take a girl for a drive, and he is stuck on you. We have witnesses to that. You can smear some dirt on yourself and say you jumped in time. It will be quick and clean. They won't even be suspicious of you."

Convincing her took a long time. He had to remind her, without being too obvious, that her own safety was tied up with his. That she was in too deep to get out if she wanted to. That there was no other way but this. And all the time he had to fight down his own furious anger and sound sweetly reasonable. At length she sighed and nodded.

"All right, Marc. Whatever you say."

He sat beside her while she called Smitty at his hotel. She followed instructions exactly, telling the gunman to go down to the lobby and call her back from a pay phone, so there would be no danger of switchboard eavesdropping. They waited together, in silence, until the phone rang again.

She went through the routine, just as Henderson

had told her. He sat beside her, his ear close to the receiver, and was shocked to hear Smitty's flat refusal.

"No," Smitty said. "I buy out. I want no part of that wild man if he knows he is being crossed."

Henderson knew he should have anticipated that. The whole thing was a business deal with Smitty, a matter of balancing the profit again the risks. The girl did not have the hold over him Henderson himself would have had. Henderson reached out and took the receiver.

"Don't be so hasty," he said. "Do you know who you are talking to?" And he laughed, a dry chuckle he had deliberately cultivated as a mannerism of "Henderson."

Even as he spoke he knew it was insane. Much better to have cut his losses and run than to let Smitty know he was still alive. He had let this obsession with Grogan, for killing Grogan, destroy his reason. But it was done now.

"Do you know me?" he asked again.

Dead silence stretched for a long moment. Then: "I guess I do."

"Maybe you'll be more willing to do business now."

Silence again. Smitty had a new element to figure into his calculations. A big element. His fear of Henderson.

"Maybe I will," Smitty said at length: "But it's still business. What's the tag?"

Henderson was ready for that. It wouldn't do to name too high a price, that would tip Smitty off as to how desperate the situation was.

"Ten grand," he said.

"How do you figure to work it?" Smitty asked.

That was better, but there was still a cool judgment

in his tone which Henderson found disquieting.

"Call him at ten o'clock," Henderson said, "and set up a meeting. He will think he is safe while you are waiting for the money. I'll leave that part to you. At eleven my car will be parked at the first crossroads north of town. You can swing by and pick up the girl, and it will go easy from there on. Okay?"

"Will she break?" Smitty asked.

"If she would, I'd call it different. This is my neck too, you know."

Whatever Smitty's reservations, and he must have had them, he made up his mind quickly.

"Good enough," he said. "We've done business before. We never try to cross each other, do we?"

Henderson's sense of depression did not last long after he hung up. When the girl shrank back from him, looking at him almost with loathing, the idea came to him for making a profit from the change of plan. He had only needed her as a go-between with Smitty, and now the necessity for that was past. How much better for her to go over the cliff with Grogan, solving most of his problems with one gesture. Smitty would like it better, too—obviously he had been afraid she would break under cross-examination. Henderson approved of that solution very much.

The afternoon wore slowly along for both of them. The girl fidgeted, roamed restlessly about the room, but made no move to try to leave. She scrambled eggs and made coffee at dinner time, after Henderson's terse refusal to go out. She pushed the food around on her plate but ate very little. Henderson thought he saw a gradual return of her earlier suspicion. Her manner wasn't all distaste for the task ahead—she was afraid for herself. Because he did not want the showdown to come sooner than necessary, he spoke softly to her.

"Better be packing up," he said. "We may be on the move pretty soon."

That was no more than the simple truth. Before the bodies were found at the bottom of some canyon, Henderson would have to be far away. He did not dare stay to play the sorrowing relative. He did not have quite that much confidence in his disguise. Too many people had seen him here. His cherished anonymity was in serious danger.

He considered putting on the "Henderson" distinguishing tags, and decided against it. He would wear a hat, so Smitty could not notice the baldness. It would be too dark to see his complexion. He would simply leave off the spectacles. Smitty wouldn't be a permanent problem, anyway.

At eleven o'clock Henderson sat behind the wheel of his car at the crossroad he had indicated to Smitty. The girl was beside him, her heavy breathing making the only sound in the stillness of the night. She had not spoken since they started. Henderson realized he was entirely right in trusting her no further.

He was concerned, in spite of himself, with Smitty's initial reaction. He held the ten thousand dollars, in mixed bills, ready on his lap. He also held a gun, its rough grip unfamiliar in his stiff fingers. He could not control the cold fear brought on by every passing set of headlights.

The hands of the dashboard clock turned slowly around to thirty minutes after eleven. To twelve o'clock. With a mounting sense of panic, Henderson began to realize Smitty was not going to come.

CHAPTER 12

Grogan's return to his surroundings was instantaneous, with no interlude of muddle-headedness or loss of memory. One moment he was out; the next he was conscious, and fully aware of what had gone before and what had happened to him. He was being carried, with hands under his shoulders and another pair grasping him around the knees. The hands released him abruptly so that he fell jarringly against a hard surface. He had sufficient control of himself to lie limp and relaxed.

He felt a surge of terror that was new in his experience. He had been in tight places before; at least once he had not expected to get out of alive. He had thought of himself then as being afraid, but it had been nothing like this. Then he had been alone, with nothing to regret except the passing of Grogan. Now there was Betsy. Even the earlier stress of the Henderson affair had not gripped him as this did, because he had never really been able to envision himself as helpless and unable to do anything for her. He was helpless now.

"You said there wouldn't be any trouble around the hotel." Grogan didn't recognize the voice, but he knew its owner was almost hysterical.

"How could I know these apes would bungle the job?" That was Smitty speaking.

"Bungle, hell." It was a third speaker. "We did the best we could. He was too damned quick. He never gave us a chance . . ."

"I know how quick he was," Smitty said. "If I hadn't

rapped him on the head he would have had you laid out with Paul here in another second."

"You can't leave all this mess here in the . . ."

"Shut up." Of the three of them, only Smitty remained calm and in control of himself. "We've got to wait until we are sure nobody heard the shot. I doubt if it draws any cops. It was muffled in the pocket and not too loud. None of your regulars here are going to stick their noses in it, I imagine."

"Not those bums." The first man spoke again and he had calmed down a bit. Grogan thought he must be the hotel clerk. They were obviously still in the Congo. "I'm not worried about them. But you can't leave me with a dead man on my hands."

"I don't figure to. In a few minutes, we'll take the copper's car around to the alley and haul the two of them down the backstairs. That will be the end of it for you."

"I don't like it," the man who had been accused of bungling said suddenly. "It may end for him, but you and I will be riding around with a couple of stiffs. It's too risky. Why not just dump them in the alley?"

"For one thing," Smitty said, "Grogan isn't a stiff. Not yet. I just saw him twitch—I think he's coming around."

"I'll fix that in a . . ."

"Hold it! I don't want him shot if we can help it. A car accident. That's the way it's supposed to be. That won't go over if he has a bullet in him."

"You think his cop pals will buy that?"

"Maybe not, but it will be hard to prove different when they find him behind the wheel of a car run off a cliff—especially with the girl to tell how it happened."

"What about Paul?"

"I'll figure that out."

Grogan felt the thrust of a shoe against his ribs. Not a hard kick; just an exploratory gesture. He remained still. He needed time to think about "the girl".

"Sit up, lieutenant," Smitty said. "I know you're with us. Next time I'll break a couple of ribs. And careful— I've got a gun on you."

So even that was no good. Grogan opened his eyes and used the palms of his hands against the floor to push himself to a sitting position. The room wavered and rolled in front of his eyes before it steadied and he could see Smitty a few feet away, holding an automatic. The other two men were there, the hotel clerk pale and shaken. Beside the door was the motionless body of the man Grogan had shot.

"On your feet, lieutenant."

Grogan rose to one knee, staggered sideways, and fell back on his haunches. He felt he could have made it, but it might be an advantage to have Smitty think he was still punchy.

"Can't make it," he said.

"All right. Go around behind him, Joe, and tie his hands. Tight."

Grogan submitted to the rope. With that gun on him, there was no choice. Smitty would shoot if necessary; two corpses in the room would not put him in much worse of a spot than one.

"Now get him out of here," the clerk said.

"What's your big rush?" Grogan asked. "You figure Smitty here will let you run loose after watching this? He can see as well as I can you'll squeal if you get a chance."

Joe cuffed him on the side of the head, hard enough

to send him crashing back against the floor.

"God, Smitty, I wouldn't squeal...."

"Oh, shut up," Smitty said. "He's trying to save his own skin. Gag him, Joe. I've got to think."

And there he was, Grogan thought desperately, trussed up like a chicken, his jaws biting helplessly into the dirty handkerchief, his arms fastened tightly behind him. Only his legs were free, and they were probably too wobbly to stand on even if he got a chance.

"Get them out of here," the clerk said again. "Both of them. Somebody's bound to come in here sooner or later."

"We'll get to that."

"What do we do with Paul?"

"We'll figure that on the way to the mountains."

Grogan felt a certain admiration for Smitty's cold nerve. Only his calm kept the other two from going to pieces entirely.

They all jumped at the jangle of the bell from the lobby. Smitty jerked his thumb toward the door; the clerk shook his head and pressed back against the wall. His face was a pasty white. Smitty shrugged and put down the gun before walking to the door himself.

Grogan heard him say: "Sorry. No more rooms."

Another voice mumbled something. Grogan considered, and decided against, the advisability of drumming his heels on the floor. It was the only gesture he was free to make, and it didn't hold enough hope to justify the inevitable crack on the head. Smitty came back into the room.

"Get his keys out of his pocket," he said, "and go drive his car around to the alley. He'll be parked within a block or so. You know the car—that blue Olds."

"Not me." Joe was vehement. "His pals may have spotted the car, and be waiting for us. I say we're crazy to take it."

Smitty considered, and obviously decided Joe had been pushed as far as was wise for the moment. He walked over to Grogan and tested the gag; it was efficiently tight.

"All right," he said, "I'll get it myself. You keep an eye on things there. I'll be back in a couple of minutes."

After he left the room Joe went quickly to the window and peered out through the soiled curtain. The window was on the front street, and would look down almost on Grogan's Olds. Grogan worked frantically with his tongue against the gag. If he could talk to these two weak links while Smitty was out of the room, he might be able . . . But Smitty had forestalled him. The gag was solid. Grogan could only mumble unintelligibly against it.

He was stronger now. Perfectly able to gain his feet in a quick movement, if that should be necessary. He considered doing it and making a dash for the door, trusting to Joe's rattled nerves to make him miss, even if he dared risk the noise of the shot. But the door was closed, and opened inward. With his hands useless, they would be on him before he could batter his way through, and Smitty would soon be back.

Grogan decided to wait until they started loading the car. If the corpse was given priority, as seemed likely since he was unable create a disturbance, there would be only one guard in the room. That would be the time to make his try; he was determined not to let them get him into the car. His chances were small enough at present, but they would be hopeless then.

He took time for a moment's self-reproach at his idiotic refusal of a bodyguard. The great Grogan. The man who could take care of anything.

Smitty returned. Joe and the clerk looked eagerly at him; he shrugged and polished his hands together in a motion of satisfaction.

"Like a dream," he said. "We're in the alley, right by the back door. I unscrewed the bulb so it's as dark as all hell. I unlocked the trunk. You two haul Paul down and stow him away in the trunk. We'll let the lieutenant ride up front."

"Not me," the clerk said. "I wouldn't touch that for a million dollars."

Smitty's smooth features turned really ugly for the first time. He crossed the room and slapped the clerk viciously across the face. Red welts stood out on the pasty complexion. Then, as the clerk shrank back against the wall without attempting a defense, Smitty slapped him twice more.

"You'll touch what I tell you," Smitty said. "You think I would leave you alone here with Grogan? Even tied up, he could eat you for breakfast. Pick up those feet and get moving, or you'll ride in the trunk yourself."

The clerk's fear of Smitty was greater than his repugnance at touching the corpse. He stooped and grasped the dead thug's feet; Joe put his hands under the shoulders and lifted. Smitty opened the door, peered outside into the hall, and motioned them through. When he closed the door behind them he shrugged.

"Not much to work with," he said. "Rather have you with me than against me, lieutenant. We could have made a team. Well, that's the way she bounces."

Grogan mumbled against the gag and tried to

indicate by motions of his head that he wanted to speak. Smitty laughed.

"Nothing to talk about, lieutenant. I'm trying to decide whether I can trust you to walk down to the car, or if it would be smarter to give you another crack on the head. I'm afraid that's going to be the answer, even if you are heavier than hell."

For all his casual confidence, Smitty remained across the room from Grogan, and he kept his automatic in his hand. It was steady as a rock. Any attempt on Grogan's part would have been suicide. He cursed to himself and wished he had made his try while Smitty had been gone.

When the two unwilling pallbearers returned, the clerk looked white and sick, and even Joe wore an expression of pained repugnance.

"He's in," Joe said. "Christ, what a lousy job."

The bell in the hall lobby was rung vigorously. Smitty darted a glance at his two henchmen; it was clear that neither of them was in a state to answer it. He looked down at Grogan, speculatively. The bell jangled again.

"Stand right by the lieutenant's head," Smitty told Joe. "Crack him a good one if he moves a muscle. This is no time for any noise."

Smitty waited until Joe took up the designated position. Then he tucked the automatic into his hip pocket, where the loose tail of his flowered sports shirt concealed it. He walked to the door, a picture of casual unconcern.

"No rooms left tonight," they heard him say, his voice muffled by the closed door.

"You the owner here?"

There was nothing muffled about those booming

tones. Grogan felt a flashing exultation. Bill Mallory.

Grogan rolled sideways, thumping his heels against the floor as he rolled. He felt a raking blow across the scalp as Joe chopped down with his pistol barrel, but the twisting movement had deflected his aim. Grogan swiveled around on his back, jackknifing his legs. Pain coursed through his shoulder as Joe struck and missed the target again. Then Grogan kicked out with both feet, sending Joe crashing back against the wall.

Gunfire roared from the hall. Joe straightened up and looked down his sights at Grogan, while the clerk cowered at the far end of the room, completely out of the picture. Grogan rolled sideways again and brought his feet under him to jump to a standing position. Joe shot twice, hastily, and missed both times.

The door was smashed open. Grogan saw Joe turn, gun ready, his eyes wide and frightened. One shot boomed from the doorway and Joe lurched forward. The clerk screamed, a high, meaningless sound. Then Bill Mallory was cutting Grogan's bonds.

"We drew that out a little fine," Mallory observed. "Sorry we lost you for a while, Steve."

"I was damned glad to see you when you came."

"Yeah. Well, does this wind it up?"

Grogan sighed. Events of the last hour had allowed him little time for deductive thinking, but one fact stood out.

"No," Grogan said. "This bunch was just out to kill me. They weren't interested in money. They didn't even talk about the pay-off. That can only mean one thing. Morrison had it wrong, somehow. Henderson is still alive."

CHAPTER 13

Grogan sat with Bill Mallory in the Chief's office, waiting for the call to Inspector Morrison to come through.

"Sorry I didn't get there sooner," Mallory said. "I had your phone bugged, but I didn't want to follow you too close. We didn't hear the shot, so we didn't know you were in trouble. When your pals moved your car and carried the body down, I figured it was time to move in."

Mallory lit his pipe and twisted himself to a position of greater comfort in his swivel chair. His stolid, unimaginative presence was a comfort to Grogan. This was the sort of man he was accustomed to working with, the sort he understood. Being with him was better than the lone wolf act.

"You still figure Henderson must be alive?" Mallory asked.

"It has to be that way. Why hasn't that call to Morrison come through yet?"

Mallory smiled his first smile of the night. "Maybe he's sleeping too soundly to hear the phone. Have you figured out what time it is back there?"

"He's used to that."

The phone on Mallory's desk rang. He picked up the receiver, listened for a moment, said, "Okay," and handed the receiver to Grogan. "The Inspector," he said.

"Hello, sir," Grogan said. "Did I wake you up?"

"You know you did." Inspector Morrison was matter-of-fact. "I take it this is important."

"It is to me. How certain were you on the identification of that body you thought was Henderson's?"

The moment's silence was eloquent. "Not entirely satisfactory," the Inspector said finally. "As I told you, the face was ruined. Same with the bridgework. We got some prints, and they matched others we picked up from an apartment Henderson formerly occupied. You know, he had never been booked. The size was about right, and the body carried Henderson's billfold. So we figured it for Henderson. Why?"

"Because there was an attempt to kill me tonight. That doesn't add, if Henderson is dead."

"No, it doesn't." Morrison's voice quickened. "Did you get the triggerman?"

"All three of them."

"All right." Silence again, while the Inspector thought it over. "We'll get back on it, Steve. Why don't you come home?"

"Maybe. In a few days." Grogan wasn't prepared to discuss that, but there was something else he wanted to get across. "When you find Henderson, I'll be there for the trial. I guarantee it."

He didn't add: "If you find him before I do, and there is a trial," but the reservation was uppermost in his mind. Morrison sensed something of the sort.

"Stay out of it, Steve, unless you work with me. I mean that."

"Sure. So long now, sir. From here on we would just be wasting the taxpayer's money." Grogan cradled the phone.

"Well?" Mallory said.

"They don't really know. All they have is a body." Grogan repeated the New York end of the conversation. "I figure it like this. Henderson got wind of Kicker Jenson's deal with me, and rubbed him out. Quietly, hoping the body wouldn't be found. Then he picked one of his stooges, one without a record, who matched him for size, and made him the fall guy. Along with Small and DeCarlo, who probably killed Jenson for him. When his own death was established, he sent Smitty after me."

"Why? Why not just let it lie? You think he was after the money?"

"Not primarily. His plan was to make me think Jenson had knocked him off the way I wanted. I would have been damned suspicious if Jenson hadn't come around to collect."

They looked at each other, their thoughts running in the same pattern. Mallory put it into words.

"But sometime between Smitty contacting you the other night and his attempt to kill you tonight, Henderson found out you had heard of Jenson's death. Smitty didn't try to bluff it through or just drop out of the picture—he tried to kill you. But how did Henderson know that you knew Jenson was dead?"

"Could there be a leak in your department?"

Mallory frowned. "Hell, Steve, you know I can't be a hundred percent sure. No chief ever could, with a department this size. I just don't believe any of my men are tied in with the Henderson mob."

Grogan didn't think so either. He couldn't forget Smitty's voice, saying: "Especially with the girl to tell how it happened." So a girl had been working with them. And two girls had been in the room when he received that phone call which told him of the finding of Jenson's body. Three girls, counting Vic. Grogan thought about that and discarded the idea. Most certainly not Vic.

"All right, Bill," he said. "The 'how' doesn't matter, anyway. The thing we have to face is that it is going to be open season on me from now on. The kid gloves are off. He will be out to kill me anyway he can."

"That means the child will be in greater danger around you than she would alone," Mallory said. "I agree, he's through trying to scare you and intends to shut your mouth. I think you'd better get back to the big town, Steve."

"Maybe. You're probably right, but I figure I have at least a day before he can get a new crew out here. He wouldn't want to recruit locals, and it will take time for him to get the word."

Grogan was startled at that. He very much doubted the possibility, and said so. Henderson, except for the one time that his explosive temper caused his foot to slip, had always operated in the background. He would not be on the spot himself.

"Just the same," Mallory said, "we had better comb the town for him. Give me a rundown on his appearance.

When Grogan described Henderson, he was impressed again with the shadowy picture he had of the man. They had talked only twice. He was swarthy, slight of frame, with curly brown hair. There was nothing which really made Henderson stand out from the crowd, or that was in any way different from a thousand others. Finding Henderson, if he really chose to disappear, would be difficult.

"Steve," Mallory said earnestly, "I think you had better go back. I know what you've got in mind—you want to get your hands on Henderson before the law does. I don't say I wouldn't agree, if you had a chance to make it. But you don't. You're out in the open, a sitting pigeon. They can hit you from any angle, and you won't have a chance. I would do what I could, but I think Morrison can look after you better."

Grogan felt old and very, very tired. He had one clue that Mallory knew nothing about. "The girl to tell how it happened." That was something he wanted to explore alone. He stood up and held out his hand.

"Goodnight, Bill. I'll be getting back now. Thanks for everything."

"I was glad of the chance." Mallory shook hands awkwardly. "You've got my advice, Steve, but that doesn't mean I'm not with you whatever you decide. I'll leave a crew on duty out at the Carillon tonight."

Driving home, Grogan felt more alone than he had ever been in his life. There was truth in Mallory's words. "That means the child will be in greater danger around you than she would be alone." He shook his head in silent protest, but he couldn't shake away the cold fact. He was, from this moment on, a liability to Betsy. Until this struggle to the death was finished between Henderson and himself, Betsy could be looked after better by others than by Grogan.

For the first time in three years they would be separated, and he had only a few hours to make the best possible plan for her future safety. And to plan the life she would have if events took the wrong turn.

Grogan parked the Olds on the dark side of the building which held the bar. He skirted the flood-lighted parking lot as he made his way through the shadows toward the cabana. He thought it was too soon for more trouble, but he would not let his self-assurance trap him again. He felt a lost aloneness he had not known since the night of Lynn's death.

CHAPTER 14

Grogan entered the cabana at twelve-thirty. Rocco and Vic were waiting up for him; Grogan dropped into a chair.

"A trap," he said. "They tried to kill me."

He gave them an exact account of the evening, except that he did not repeat Smitty's remark concerning "the girl." They listened without interruption.

"It's all completely insane," Vic said at the end. "I don't understand."

"Simple enough," Rocco said. "Somehow, they got word Steve knew about finding Jenson's body. They were sure he wouldn't pay off. So they had orders to kill him. Henderson must still be alive."

"Oh, no," Vic's protest was a low moan. "Not that, all over again. It doesn't necessarily mean Henderson, does it Steve?"

Grogan shrugged. "Not much doubt. These were hired guns. They wouldn't have mixed up in this for the fun of it. Someone was paying them, and only Henderson would care enough. We have to figure it that way."

Involuntarily, and at the same moment, they all looked toward the bedroom. Grogan thought Vic turned more pale; his own muscles tensed. Only Rocco gave no sign of emotion.

"I don't think Betsy figures in it from now on," Grogan said. "Henderson crossed off the possibility of a deal by trying to kill me. From now on that will be what he wants, unless he drops it right here."

"You think he might do that, Steve?" Vic asked. "Drop

it, I mean?"

"It's possible. Not likely, though, and I'm going to have to get Betsy out of the line of fire. The four of us separate in the morning."

When Vic started to speak, Rocco silenced her with a gesture. The dark little man was watching Grogan intently. "What's the pitch, Steve?" he asked.

"I want you two to take Betsy downtown to a hotel. You will be there with her all the time, and I'll have Mallory put a guard in the corridor. She will be safe there until this is over."

"And you?"

"I'll need to move around a little. Don't worry. I know now what to look for, and I won't be an easy target this time. I'm more apt to get my man than he is to nail me, and I'll take him alive and talking. Then we will know where we stand."

Grogan had thought it all out during the drive from the police station. His mind was made up; he was sure this was the best course of action. He was prepared for Rocco's slow nod of acceptance. Only Vic's reaction was a surprise.

"You really are crazy, aren't you, Steve?" she asked vehemently. "Be quiet, Rocco, and don't interrupt me. There are things I have to say. Yes, Betsy will be very safe, while you go on playing this game between yourself and Henderson. Sure you are 'more apt to nail him.' For God's sake, Steve! Haven't you given a thought to the chance you take of losing? I've told you this before. There is more to keeping Betsy safe than preventing a kidnapping. Where would she be without you? Alone, growing up an orphan? A poor little rich girl with people only interested in her money. Think about it, Steve. Where will she be if you are killed?"

Grogan was overwhelmed by the intensity of her emotion. "I don't see any other . . ."

"You don't see because you won't look. Your pride is hurt. A criminal has put one over on the great Lieutenant Grogan. He won't go and hide in a hotel with his daughter, where they would both be safe, because he wants to prove he can handle any problem himself. All right, go ahead. I just ask that you realize what you are doing, that you face up to it. Don't tell me there is no other way, because I don't believe it, and I won't give you the satisfaction of deceiving yourself."

Vic dominated the room, her usually quiet eyes sparkling fire. The contempt in her glance was withering as it swept from Grogan to Rocco, daring either of them to contradict her. She continued, more quietly.

"Perhaps I am the only one of us willing to give up something important for Betsy's happiness. I'm willing to give up Betsy herself. I've decided to give her up. I wish to God nothing more was asked of me than to live with her."

Vic leaned back in her chair, her firmly closed lips an indication that she had said all she intended for the moment. She watched Grogan steadily.

"We can't hide forever." Grogan was defensive.

"You could if necessary." Vic spoke now without surface emotion. "Only it wouldn't be forever, and you know it. All the police in the country will be looking for Henderson. That massacre in the east, where he killed at least four men to make you think he was dead, will turn his gang from him. Especially after what happened out here tonight, he won't be able to trust a soul for help. They'll get him. Maybe a week, maybe a month, maybe five years. But they will get him. What criminal, wanted as he is, has ever held out for long?"

One part of Grogan's mind wanted to argue with her. There had seldom been another wanted criminal quite so faceless, so unknown, as Henderson. Seldom a wanted man where the authorities had so little idea of just what they were after. On the other hand, why did he think he alone could be successful? Because he was "the great Lieutenant Grogan?" It could be the answer. Grogan was deeply shocked when he realized the truth of that.

He got up from his chair and walked down the hall to Betsy's room. He eased the door open and stood just inside, looking down at the small figure in the twin bed. As he watched her Grogan remembered her mother's voice, coming from a long-ago time before their marriage. Lynn had been fiercely insistent.

"I won't have you say you have nothing to offer me, Steve," she had said. "You have yourself—your stubborn, dependable self, who loves me just because I'm me. You talk about your background. Think of mine for a moment. Alone in some school, because there was no place else for me. Alone at a camp, summers, because no one wanted the bother of having me underfoot. Now that I have you, do you think I'll let you escape?"

Grogan sighed. Betsy stirred in her sleep; Grogan froze silently in the doorway while she turned over, groped with one hand for the rag doll, and settled back to sleep. Then he tiptoed out of the room, closing the door quietly behind him.

Vic and Rocco remained as he had left them. Grogan went to stand beside Vic, resting his hand on her shoulder. She looked up at him, unwaveringly.

"Thanks," he said. "A man just doesn't think straight, sometimes. When he most needs to, usually."

"Steve, I didn't mean . . ."

"You meant what you said, and you were right. It was something I needed to hear. You've been right all along, but it's too late to change the past now. From here on in I'll do what I can."

"You call it, Steve."

It was Rocco who spoke. Vic answered him only with her eyes. They were shining through a film of tears. Grogan sat down again, feeling drained, empty, but more content than he had before.

"I see it this way," he said. "We will make no move tonight. I'm positive we're safe for twenty-four hours. It'll take at least that long for Henderson, wherever he is, to get word of what happened here. Maybe he will try for me again and maybe he won't, but we'll figure it as though he would.

"We won't go east yet. If we hole up downtown in the hotel, Mallory can give us all the protection we could get in New York, and I think he has a better chance of picking up the boys Henderson may send after me. They'll be strangers. Henderson couldn't get local talent for this job. I won't make a move. I promise you that. Hell, I promise myself that."

"How long will we stay here?" Vic asked. She was quiet—she was leaving the decisions in his hands again.

"Just for a few weeks. If nothing has happened by then, we will try to make permanent plans. With whatever safeguards seem best at the time. Okay?"

"Yes, Steve. Oh, yes."

"I think so myself, Steve," Rocco said, unexpectedly.

"Now one more thing," Grogan said. "I have a sort of a clue, one I didn't mention to Mallory. I'll tell him first thing in the morning. I might as well see what you think now."

He told them about Smitty's revealing disclosure. Vic gasped. Rocco leaned forward, a cat ready to spring, his dark face predatory.

"So that's how they knew," he said. "One of the dames here when you got the call. One of the two. Which of them was it, Steve?"

Grogan shrugged. He was reluctant to believe it of either. He looked at Vic.

"I don't know," she said slowly. "Not even which one to suspect. They both seem sweet girls."

"You can't figure it that way," Rocco said. "They both got here right after we came. Didn't the Kelley kid open at the club the day after we registered?"

"Yeah." Grogan was reluctant. "Pretty quick, but not too quick if we were spotted all the time. It's possible. I admit that. Did you see anything of the people next door tonight?"

"Their lights were on until just before you got home," Vic said. "The radio was playing. We didn't see them."

Grogan drummed his fingers on the arm of his chair. When he spoke his words were reluctant, and not at all in his usual decisive style.

"It's too late to brace Liza tonight," he said. "What would you think if I went over to the club to see Terry? If she had a part in this, she isn't tough enough not to be shaken. At least, I don't think she is. I might spot something."

Somewhat to his surprise, Vic nodded. He didn't even wonder to see himself waiting for Vic's approval before starting a course of action. Grogan, who had never waited for anyone's opinion.

"It might be a good idea," she said.

"I'll make it safe," Rocco said. "I'll tag along."

Grogan did not protest. He had done things his way for a long time, and had made a mess of it. He was willing to listen to advice.

It was only a little after one as they went up the pathway toward the club—the high point of the evening for the Casa Carillon. Screams of laughter came to them from the flood-lighted pool. The club itself was having a crowded night, judging from the cars jammed into the parking lot. The music of the three-piece orchestra drifted through the open doorway.

Grogan felt himself a Judas for what he was about to do. He did not really suspect Terry of any complicity with Henderson; her bright innocence made the idea unthinkable. With anything other than Betsy's welfare at stake, he would not have considered it for a moment. As things were, he felt he had no choice. Yet just by walking through that door, intending to judge her for a guilty reaction, he knew he was putting a barrier between them. Whether she was innocent or guilty, the result to their personal relationship would be the same.

Memory of Betsy, small, helpless, unbelievably dear Betsy, hardened his resolve. This was a possible approach to her safety. He wasn't going to turn away from it.

The music had stopped before they entered, and the bandstand was empty. Grogan, from force of habit and because of its safe anonymity, headed directly for the far booth at the rear of the room. Rocco stopped at the bar, taking an empty stool at the front end. He put his back to the bar and let his eyes wander over the room.

A bartender brought Grogan a beer; he started to speak, glanced again at Grogan, and changed his mind. He went back to the bar, leaving Grogan brooding behind him.

Pop came out of the men's room and walked to the bandstand, the other two musicians straggling after him. No sign of Terry. They settled down to their instruments, Pop tapped his foot twice, and the music began. Grogan sat watching the dancers mill about the tiny floor, only half-seeing them, as his mind groped with the problem of Terry's absence. She was always in her chair on the stand between her numbers, unless she was back at the table with him.

At the end of the last chorus Pop peered down the smoky room toward Grogan's booth. He laid down his saxophone, stepped from the stand, and approached Rocco at the bar. They talked quietly together for a moment.

When Pop left Rocco, he did not return to the bandstand but picked his way the length of the room, shaking off an occasional hand as a patron tried to detain him. A group at a table near the front began a rhythmic clapping, demanding more music. The rest of the crowd took it up, mingling it with good-natured calls to Pop. The big man continued stolidly toward Grogan. He paused at the rear booth and leaned over, resting the palms of his hands on the table.

"A tough night," Pop said.

Grogan didn't answer. The words he knew he should speak stuck in his throat.

"I suppose you're looking for Terry," Pop said.

"Yeah. Sort of."

"I gave her the night off. Her old man is in town,

and he isn't feeling so good. She's been looking after him all day. She called me about six, and I told her she didn't need to show tonight. The boss is sore as hell."

Grogan sat looking up at Pop for a long moment while the words he had just heard sank down and down inside him. Pop stared back at him, then he turned toward the bandstand and nodded his head. The music of the bull fiddle and the piano started immediately. Pop seated himself in the booth opposite Grogan.

"You look beat, Steve," Pop said.

That was no word for it, Grogan thought. He didn't want to talk or explore the matter at all; he just wanted to go away quietly. And yet he knew he had to find out what there was to know. Warily, of course. If Terry wasn't on the level, then Pop probably couldn't be trusted either. Suspecting the big, respectable-looking musician was difficult.

"I've had a hard day," Grogan said. "I'd like to talk to Terry. You know where she is?"

Pop shook his head. "She didn't say. Just that her old man was here, and sick, and she needed to stay with him."

"Funny she didn't bring him to her place here."

"Not so funny. Hell, he's not sick, he's drunk. I've known Mike Kelley for twenty years. She wouldn't want him around lousing up the job for her. And she might not want him around you."

"So you're telling me."

"Yeah, I'm telling you." Pop scowled at Grogan. "And not because I give a damn about you either, if you'll excuse the frankness. I'm thinking about Terry. If her old man being a drunk is too much for you, better you find it out now and let her alone. I told you before, Grogan, I don't intend to see Terry hurt."

"All right, all right. My own old man was a drunk, as far as that goes. I'm used to them."

"She doesn't see much of him, anyway. He's been a drifter for the last four, five years. I haven't met him myself for at least five years."

"Why 'drifter'?" Grogan asked. "Maybe he straightened out, turned respectable."

Pop grunted. "Not Mike Kelley. Not that punch-drunk pug. Oh, hell, maybe not punch-drunk. He can be a sweet enough guy, sober. But no good. No good for Terry."

"What does he look like? When you last saw him, I mean."

"Huh?" Pop was surprised. "What's that got to do with it?"

"I just want to know. You're gabby enough about everything else."

It was a crazy thought. The idea that Terry's long-missing father might be Henderson. Henderson's history had gone back about five years. Before that only blankness.

"He looked like anybody else. In the chips, with good clothes, he might be gentleman Irish. He didn't look like a bum, if that's what you mean. Probably doesn't now, after he sobers up. Are you choosy about how your father-in-law looks, Grogan?"

"Just curious. How big is he?"

Pop acted as though he were humoring a lunatic. "Middle-sized," Pop said. "No bigger than that. Nothing special about his face one way or the other."

"Any marks of the ring on him?"

"Hell, yes. Scarred eyebrows. One thick ear. Quite a

bit worse than yours."

Which meant little or nothing, of course. Plastic surgery could change all that. Grogan felt that Pop was right, that he really was crazy, building up a case with no more to go on than that.

"What color hair?" he asked.

"Hair? Bald as an eagle. Has been for years. What's eating on you, Grogan?"

"Nothing. You started talking about the old man and I'm willing to go along. He means nothing to me."

Pop heaved himself to his feet. "He don't mean a hell of a lot to me, either. I came back to talk to you about Terry, and she's what I'm interested in. You know now where I stand. I'll be getting back to work."

Grogan stood up too. He and Pop were of a height; they stared steadily at each other, a hint of belligerency on both faces.

"I know where you say you stand," Grogan said. "If it checks out, I'll shake hands with you someday. If you're lying to me, just remember I can be a rough sort of guy myself."

He watched closely for a reaction to that. If Pop knew what was going on, he would know it was an open threat and a plainly-voiced suspicion. With three men already dead that night, Pop would have to be a tough operator to stand up to it without hesitation.

Pop was either exactly that or an innocent man. Grogan saw nothing but a quick flare of animosity, followed by puzzlement. Grogan had never used that tone to him before.

"Forget it," Grogan said. "You want to shake hands?"

"We'll let that ride awhile. I've got some things to figure out."

Pop turned and walked toward the bandstand.

Grogan waited a moment, then followed him through the crowd to where Rocco waited at the end of the bar. He and Rocco went outside together.

Grogan woke in the morning to find Betsy tugging at his hair. She was bright-eyed and alert, her face glowing with mischief.

"I want my daddy to get up," she said. "I want my daddy to fix my breakfast."

"All right, sugar."

Grogan felt a relaxation of the tension. He had problems, certainly, but they didn't loom as blackly forbidding as they had before. Not with Betsy, the prize he was playing for, so clearly safe and untouched. He was even able to shrug off the memory of the suspicion he had displayed and must continue to display toward Terry. None of it was important compared to Betsy.

"Come on," Betsy said. "Hurry up." She was imperious.

"Go and let Vic dress you, while daddy takes a shower," Grogan said. "Then we'll see about breakfast."

As she ran out of the room Grogan recalled, in a quick flashback, his peril at the Congo Hotel the night before. He shuddered. He had been a damn fool. Never again.

He found Vic and Rocco both up and dressed. She was smiling almost happily, humming as she bustled about the small kitchen. Rocco gave Grogan one of his rare smiles.

"What's the program?" Rocco asked.

"I'll call Mallory and set up the move."

He was able to reach the police chief at home. Mallory listened without comment while Grogan told him things he had left out the night before. Grogan was explicit about his suspicions, including Terry's staying away from work.

"As I see it," Grogan finished, "it had to be one of the two acting as finger man. Either Liza Carrol or Terry Kelley."

"You could have told me earlier."

Mallory's voice held reserve, and a certain amount of doubt. Grogan didn't blame him.

"I was going to handle it myself. As usual. Now I've seen the light. This is your case, Bill. Yours and Morrison's. I'm bowing out. From here on I'm just the innocent taxpayer you'll have to protect."

"What's the new angle? This is quite a switch." Mallory was still skeptical.

"I just realized something. I'm a taxpayer with a daughter, and I'm going to stick to her. Not on the firing line, but holed up where we'll both be safe."

"If you really mean that, you couldn't have come to a better decision." Mallory sounded entirely friendly now. "But you shouldn't stay out at the Carillon. It's too open for real protection."

"That's right. We want to move into a hotel this morning. Pick one for us, will you? A suite big enough for the four of us, one you can sew up tight. I'll leave it in your hands, Bill."

"Good enough. Just sit still, and I'll be out in an hour. By then I may be able to get a line on where this singer is staying."

Betsy prattled happily throughout breakfast, doing the talking for all of them. Afterward she bustled behind Vic, giving three-year-old's assistance to the packing. She had become infected with Vic's happiness, and was hilariously gay. Grogan sat beside the front window, watching the walk until he saw Bill Mallory approaching from the parking lot, flanked by two bulky men.

Mallory came in alone, leaving the two officers outside. They were joined by a third man from a cabana two doors to the south, on the opposite side from the Carrol place. Grogan had not known before that their guard had been staying there.

"Ready to go?" Mallory asked.

"Any time. But just the others first, Bill. No point to putting all your eggs in one basket, when I'm the egg they're after. I think it's too soon for trouble, but still . . ."

"Right. I'll stay here with you until they get set."

It was arranged that way. Betsy at first refused to go anywhere without her daddy. Then, her mercurial attention attracted by Vic's description of the hotel, she kissed him casually and was impatient to be off. Grogan squeezed her wriggling little body and managed to land a kiss on her right ear.

He watched them go to the parking lot. Betsy skipped along beside Vic, holding her hand. One of the detectives led the way by ten yards, another kept just beside them. Rocco brought up the rear. Grogan sighed. It was the safest procedure he could possibly imagine, it was the result of careful thought rather than intuition, and it was concurred in by others who were in a position to reason more clearly than he. Yet he didn't like it. Every instinct urged him to snatch Betsy up and drive away, far away, alone with her. He lit a cigarette and turned to Mallory. Instinct hadn't gotten him far on this affair to date.

"I found where the Kelley girl is staying," Mallory said. "The Green Grotto Motel, two blocks up the street. At least, a fellow who signed as Mike Kelley checked in there yesterday."

"What sort of a place is it?"

"A dump. You wouldn't stay there if you could afford anything else. I haven't checked Kelley out yet."

Mallory walked to the door and beckoned the remaining detective. He came in, a lean, blond fellow Grogan had not noticed before. Mallory introduced him as Harris.

"We're interested in this cabin next door," Mallory said. "Guy named Bragg with his daughter. You see anything of them last night?"

Harris shook his head. "They were home, I think. The lights were on and the radio playing, anyhow. That doesn't mean much. They could have slipped in and out on me, and I might not have spotted them. I've never seen the man, anyway. I would remember the woman, I guarantee that."

"This shouldn't take us long," Mallory told Grogan. "Now that you can pin it down pretty much to the two girls, we'll just backtrack them. I'll go see both of them as soon as I get you settled."

Grogan nodded, only a small part of his attention on the conversation. He was listening for the telephone with every nerve straining. That short drive downtown for Betsy was looming in his mind as the most important journey in the world, and the most dangerous. If he had it to do again, he would never have let her go without him. He leaped for the phone before the first ring died away.

"All okay, Steve," Rocco told him. "Not a hitch."

Relief flooded Grogan. "Good boy," he said. "I'll be along soon."

"Now then, Steve," Mallory said, "maybe I should

run you downtown to join the flock and get on about my business."

"I guess so."

Mallory shot him a quick look. "You want to go with me, Steve? To talk to the women, and the men with them? It's going to be sticky. At least one is a legitimate father-daughter relationship, and that girl isn't going to feel complimented by the questions we'll have to ask."

"That's not the problem. I'll go if you think it is the thing to do. I'm following your advice. I told you it was your case, and I mean it."

Mallory scratched his head. Neither of them acknowledged the incongruity of Steve Grogan questing so carefully for the safe course to follow.

"You would be a help," Mallory said. "You know them, could judge their reactions better. And I don't see why it wouldn't be perfectly safe. They couldn't start anything on the spot."

"All right."

Grogan's spirits rose. This could be nothing on his conscience, since Mallory had suggested it, and it gave him a chance to have a hand in the proceedings.

"I talked to Morrison this morning," Mallory said. "He's convinced Henderson is still alive. He has the wires humming. He's anxious for a capture, too, not a killing. After all this, Henderson hasn't a prayer of getting off; if he talks, the Inspector will be able to tie up some loose ends on the others."

Grogan nodded insincerely. He was not interested in taking Henderson alive for the tying up of loose ends. He wanted Henderson dead, and if Grogan had a hand in it that was the way things would be. He wished there was more of a chance for finding the man here.

"Which one will we see first?" Grogan asked.

"Might as well start next door. Kelley and the singer are being watched. They can't get away."

Discussing it in that prosaic, manhunting manner set Grogan's nerves on edge. Still, there was no point to being squeamish. It had to be done, and he was the logical one to be there when the questions were asked. He was glad they were starting with Liza Carrol.

"Come on, then," Grogan said. "We'll get the show on the road."

CHAPTER 15

Mallory stepped in front of Grogan to ring the bell next door. Harris halted a few paces behind them, leaning against the side of the porch. It had been agreed that he was to remain outside. Mallory rang twice more before the door opened.

John Bragg, wearing a dressing gown, eyed them quizzically. He was freshly shaved; the pasty complexion gave him the appearance of illness. He passed a hand over his bald head.

"Yes?" he said. Then, noting Grogan he became more cordial. "Good morning, Mr. Grogan. I didn't see you at first."

"I'm Mallory, of the city force," Mallory said brusquely. He gave Grogan no chance to speak. "John Bragg?"

"That's right." Bragg seemed puzzled.

"I would like to talk to you for a few minutes."

"Of course, of course. Come on in." Bragg stepped to one side.

There was no trace of Liza in the room. Mallory, hunched over in the chair Bragg offered him, dominated the gathering. He was a hulking figure in his wrinkled suit and scuffed shoes. His shirt, even so early in the morning, was rumpled, his tie pulled slightly to one side. He was a movie version of a flatfoot, Grogan thought resentfully. And yet there was an acuteness about him that inspired confidence. No one would ever make the mistake of considering Bill Mallory stupid.

"Is your daughter here?" Mallory asked.

He made it somewhat peremptory. Bragg frowned, glanced at Grogan, and smoothed his expression to affability.

"She isn't feeling well this morning," he said. "A slight headache, I believe. She is still in bed."

"I'll need to talk to her, please."

Bragg shrugged and stood up. "I will see how she feels. I presume you gentlemen will have some adequate explanation for all this." He sounded as though he were controlling his irritation with difficulty.

Bragg disappeared into one of the bedrooms. Grogan frowned at Mallory. The policeman grinned at him. They could hear low-voiced conversation from the bedroom, without being able to distinguish the words.

When Bragg returned Liza followed close behind him. She had not been in bed recently, Grogan was sure. Although she wore a negligee and slippers, her hair was carefully arranged and obviously some time had been expended on her make-up. She was pale but composed.

"Hello, Steve," she said. Both her tone and her smile were friendly.

"These gentlemen seem to be here officially," John Bragg said grimly. "My dear, this is Mr. Mallory, a policeman."

Grogan and Mallory had risen when she entered the room. Mallory made no attempt at social ease; he stood scowling and truculent for a moment, then sat down again. Grogan waited until Liza and John Bragg were seated before he resumed his chair. Seeing her this way, his suspicions seemed fantastic.

"An attempt was made to kill Mr. Grogan last night," Mallory said abruptly.

Grogan was watching Liza. Her eyes widened and her hand fluttered to her throat. When he turned to Bragg, the man was frowning.

"What does that have to do with us?" Bragg asked. "We are sorry, of course, but . . ."

"Maybe nothing," Mallory said. "This is just routine. A girl was mixed up in it, and Mr. Grogan doesn't know too many girls in this town. I'm asking all his friends where they were last night."

That brought life to Liza's pale mask. Color glowed on her cheeks as she looked at Grogan.

"Steve, you can't think that I . . ."

"I'm doing the thinking," Mallory said. "Where were you last night, Mrs. Carrol?"

"My daughter and I did not leave the house all evening," John Bragg said. "I don't suppose I can prove it. Really, Sergeant, this is outrageous."

The words were calm enough, but Grogan saw the pulse throbbing at temple and throat, and knew suddenly that they were looking at a man of violent temper. A man who was unaccustomed to being crossed. He considered and discarded a ridiculous thought. Bragg was older than Henderson, slighter, and there was nothing fake about his baldness. The eyes were different, too.

"I'm the Chief, not a sergeant," Mallory said. "No offense intended. As I say, I'm asking everybody. What's your line of business, Mr. Bragg?"

"Hardware dealer. Retired." The words were clipped and controlled.

"Where do you live?"

"Newark, New Jersey. My daughter and I have been traveling for several months. I can't begin to understand what all this . . ."

"Mr. Bragg," Mallory said patiently, "I'm sure you can understand if you give the matter some thought. I know nothing about you people except what you tell me, and obviously I can't take your word for that. I will have to verify every scrap of information you give me about your background. Not just you—I'm doing it for everyone concerned. If you aren't the ones I'm after, and probably you aren't, you will receive a full apology. Meantime, I will treat you with such courtesy as you permit."

"For heaven's sake, tell him what he wants to know. What harm can it do?"

Liza sounded close to tears. Grogan tried to catch her eye, but she refused to look at him. Well, he thought, what else could you expect? He hadn't counted on her cheering over his part in this.

Mallory pulled out a notebook and took Bragg through a recital of his addresses, business connections, and acquaintances over a period of years. The answers came through mounting tension, as the man struggled with increasingly obvious exasperation. However, he kept his temper to the end, replying without hesitation to Mallory's probings. Only when the policeman started to go over the same ground did he rebel.

"I think that is enough," he said. "You wanted facts to check, now you have them. I don't intend to sit here while you try to trip me up on some trivial detail. You had better leave now, Mr. Mallory."

Mallory shrugged. "As you wish. After I have some of the same sort of information from Mrs. Carrol."

Liza told her story with more faltering and groping than her father had done. She repeated herself, contradicted herself on dates, was exceedingly hazy as to names and addresses. Mallory wrote patiently in his notebook. Bragg watched them, making no move to interfere or help her, and except for the telltale pulse giving no indication of concern. Grogan could not convince himself that it meant anything. Most men would have been angry under the circumstances, and many women would have been confused. At length Mallory stood up.

"Thank you," he said. "That's enough for now. You've been very patient. Can I depend on your staying around until I see you again?"

"Or you will arrest us, I suppose," Liza said. She showed her first tinge of bitterness.

"I would be forced to do exactly that. Well?"

"You will find us here when you want us," Bragg said. "Gentlemen, I have been ill. I really think . . ."

"We're leaving," Mallory said. "Thank you again."

Grogan followed him out the door, not knowing what to say. There was nothing to be said, actually. However this turned out, anything which might have been between himself and Liza Carrol was ended. He found he minded only because it pointed up the inevitable result of the next interview with Terry.

"What do you think?" Mallory asked Grogan.

"All of their story might be true, or none of it. I didn't pick up anything. We just won't know for a day or so."

There lay the advantage of working through the department. In a matter of hours Mallory would have men checking the stories in a dozen cities. Alone, Grogan had no such resources.

"Now for the singer," Mallory said. "I'm sorry, Steve. Would you rather sit this one out?"

"No." Grogan realized he made it more explosive than necessary. "I'll see it through."

Leaving Harris behind with instructions to keep an eye on Liza Carrol and John Bragg, they drove two blocks to the Green Grotto Motel. Mallory was right. It was not a place which would have been chosen except through economic necessity. Paint peeled from the walls, the beaten-down patches of grass were dusty brown, the cars parked in the open stalls were battered jalopies. Grogan paid little attention to the squalor; his mind was focused on this meeting with Terry.

Mallory spoke to a man in the doorway of one of the cabins. The policeman jerked his head down the path, and said: "Number ten. Still there."

Mallory rapped on the door of number ten. Although only midmorning, the sun was blisteringly hot. Grogan felt it beating down on his shoulders as they stood there in the dust waiting for an answer from inside.

Terry opened the door almost immediately. She was wearing pedal pushers and a T shirt. Her hair was tousled; blue-black circles under her eyes emphasized the pallor of her face. Grogan's heart twisted to see her looking so tired and forlorn. And so alone. Her eyes took on a sparkle when she saw Grogan.

"Steve," she said, flashing the familiar smile. Then

she sobered as the meaning of Mallory's policeman-like bulk came to her. "Steve?" she said again, questioningly.

"Look, Terry," Grogan said, "this is something . . ."

"I'll do the talking, Grogan," Mallory said. "I'm Mallory of the city force, miss. I have some questions to ask you and your father."

"Why . . . of course. Come on in."

The cabin was a single room, with an electric plate and a sink in one corner to mark the kitchen. A man lay in the bed, propped up with pillows. He appeared to be about the size of John Bragg, and he too was bald and pale. He grinned at them as they filed into the room.

"The police," he said. "I would have known it without the introduction at the door."

"This is Mr. Mallory, dad," Terry said, her voice tight. "And Steve Grogan."

"Mike Kelley, at your service." Kelley shook the hand Grogan held out to him. "I've heard about you, Steve. I'm sobering up to meet you. You weren't expected quite yet."

"Please, dad . . ."

"This isn't a social call," Mallory said. Without invitation, he pulled a straight chair out from the kitchen table and sat down facing the bed. Grogan and Terry remained standing, with eyes only for each other. "Mr. Grogan was almost killed last night," Mallory went on. "Three other men were not so fortunate. So I'm here officially."

"Steve!"

Terry's cry was quick and spontaneous. Grogan would have staked his life on the sincerity of her anguished concern. In spite of himself he was filled with fury at Mallory's brusque manner.

"Put your minds at rest," Mike Kelley said. He was the most unconcerned person in the room. "The police have been interested in me in many cities, but this isn't one of them. And never for anything as dignified as murder, anyway. I was here with my girl all of last night, recovering from a slight indisposition."

"Just the two of you?"

"The two of us." Kelley's tone lost its lightness. "I'm not sensitive for myself, but I wouldn't like to think you were doubting my girl's word."

"There was a girl mixed up in the killing," Mallory said bluntly.

Grogan had been unable to remove his gaze from Terry's face. He saw her flinch, and her lips quivered. He set his own jaw and with an effort restrained himself from taking her in his arms.

"Now, by God, that's too much!" Kelley's deep voice was not that of a sick man. "You, there, skulking by the wall. I thought you were a friend of Terry's. Is this the way you show it, dragging the lying police here after us?" The earlier Irish lilt to his voice was gone.

"Be quiet, dad." Terry's tone was firm and controlled. "Steve, believe me, I understand that you can't completely trust anyone now. Go ahead and ask us whatever you need to know, and we'll tell you what we can."

"That's not what I say," Kelley almost bellowed. He was working himself into a rage. "I won't have them breaking in here and . . ."

"Please, dad. Please."

It quieted him. Grumbling, Mike Kelley relaxed against his pillows, biting back the words he clearly wanted to say. Mallory, matter-of-fact and possibly just a bit amused, pulled out his notebook and went to work in the same methodical pattern he had followed with John Bragg.

Listening, and weighing all the factors as carefully as he could manage, Grogan could not bring himself to decide which of the two men he believed. Kelley was less specific as to names, dates and places than Bragg had been, but the life he claimed to have led made that plausible. He had been a drifter, slipping from job to job and drink to drink much as Pop had predicated. He had not come back earlier because he wanted to "amount to something first." He looked Terry up at this time because he couldn't bear to stay away from her longer. He was pathetic, and on the surface believable. It would be a much harder story to verify than Bragg's.

Terry, in contrast, was more explicit than Liza Carrol had been. She named the times and places of her singing engagements, told the names and addresses of the people she knew in each of them, gave no indication of holding anything back. Throughout she spoke in a light, even tone which displayed no emotion. She submitted without protest to Mallory's cross-examination, and did not contradict herself on any material point. It was all very difficult for Grogan to sit through. He discovered that he was sweating even more than the hot, stuffy air of the little cabin warranted.

When Mallory at last rose to go, Grogan could hold himself in no longer. He took a step toward Terry.

"Terry," he said, "I want you to know . . ."

She stopped him with a shake of her head. "No, Steve. Not now. Later, when you are sure, we can talk. But not now."

He had no alternative to following Mallory out into the dust and heat of the driveway.

CHAPTER 16

After Grogan and Mallory left, Henderson relaxed his rigid muscles and gave way to despair. For the first time he faced the fact that he was trapped, boxed into a corner from which there was no way out. Perhaps not immediately, but in a matter of days or hours, when they began to get returns on that preposterous story he had spun for them, they would be hammering on his door.

Grogan had done it. It was Grogan, damn him, every step of the way. Grogan had started the whole thing in the first place. Grogan had drawn him into this net, made it necessary for Henderson to be on hand personally, and led him to this. Damn Grogan. He ground the knuckles of his right hand into the palm of his left, and swore to himself that however things turned out for him he would contrive to take Grogan with him. That would be some consolation.

Sound of the girl crying pulled Henderson's attention back to his immediate surroundings.

"Shut up," he said. "Sniveling isn't going to help things."

"Marc, I'm scared."

"You should be. This is a spot, a tight one. I've got to think."

"How could he know about our plans? He said 'a girl'. Where could he have heard that?"

"From Smitty, I suppose. Before they killed him he must have let something slip."

Distracted by the thought, Henderson cursed Smitty. How could he have figured on that? Smitty, the seasoned professional, had been the one to let a vital clue slip. And he still didn't understand how the police had been drawn so quickly to him. Not that they were entirely sure, as yet. If they had been, he would be under arrest. He still had a few hours, at best, until the holes in his story became apparent. "Shut up," he said again. "I need to concentrate."

She quieted down under the venom in his tone. Henderson tried to control his anger at being thwarted, tried to forget Grogan and the desire for revenge, and put his mind to the possibility of escape. It was meager.

He could do nothing under his present identity, of course; the police would be watching him too closely. His only hope lay in a return to "Henderson". They had not yet connected him with that name. Put the wig back on, and the contact lenses, darken his face, and he stood a good chance of catching the next plane out. Not with the girl. She was too spectacular, too well known. Together they would be spotted immediately.

Henderson felt more cheerful. It was never too late, if you had a brain and weren't afraid to seize your opportunities. He disliked the necessity for the plane. He would be cooped up in there, unable to get out whatever happened, gambling on the hope they would not discover his identity switch until he had landed and lost himself in a large city. He considered driving and discarded the idea. This place was too far out in the middle of nowhere, and his car was known to the police. He couldn't even steal a car. He didn't know how. In the old days it had been easy; delegate one of the boys, one familiar with the procedure of crossing ignition wires or forging keys. He consoled himself with the thought that a car would not be suitable for this country, anyway.

No, it would have to be the plane. A few hours' gamble, and if it came off, he would be safe. At least for a while. One step at a time was all he could manage now.

He crossed the room and rummaged in a drawer until he found the airline schedule he was looking for. He was conscious of the girl watching him, her face drawn with terror. He felt a moment's amused contempt.

The schedule sobered him again. No plane until evening. That meant sitting here, a rat in a trap, just hoping they would not pay him a return visit before the take-off. He didn't dare leave the cabin until shortly before the flight—that would give them that much longer to search for him. Any careless mistake would be his undoing.

"What are you going to do, Marc?" the girl asked.

"Shut up. I don't have time to quibble with you."

That was a mistake, too. He couldn't afford trouble with her during the day, while the possibility remained that the police would return to talk further with them. He couldn't have her screaming, and it wouldn't do to quiet her permanently. Not yet. She had to be made to think she had a place in the future he was planning for himself. Otherwise, she would go to pieces right then.

"I'm sorry," he said. "I've got a lot on my mind. There isn't too much time left for figuring an out to this trap. Be a good girl and let me think."

"All right, Marc."

He forced himself to sit still and hoped that he gave the impression of one lost in thought. Actually, there was nothing left to consider. He had made up his mind. Wait until the last minute, finish off the girl, disguise himself as Henderson, and make a dash for the plane. There was no other possibility.

Having decided, he was in a fury of impatience to be started, but there was nothing to do but wait. He couldn't put on the wig and the make-up too soon; Grogan might return. And he had to put up with the girl and her nerve-jarring presence. He might need her again.

After telling himself there was nothing further to consider, Henderson found he could not keep his mind off the details. The detail of silencing her, mostly. He was surprised to realize that he found the picture distasteful. In a rage, it would have been easy enough. It still shouldn't bother him; it was business, pure and simple. Still he didn't like it. Sitting there so white and frightened and still, she was somehow not a proper subject for violence. She was just another obstacle to him. The thought sent his tension mounting; he didn't like obstacles.

"Your policeman doesn't seem to be as crazy about you as you thought he was," he said. "He is willing to throw you to the wolves."

She did not answer, but her quick, veiled glance carried a look almost of satisfaction. He knew she was thinking of the safety of the child. And possibly Grogan.

He was angry enough to have choked the life out of her then and there. His fingers ached for the feel of her throat under them, and the necessity for further hours of dissembling his emotions was bitter to him.

He could not entirely hide his fury when he answered.

"Don't get the wrong idea," he said. "Maybe Grogan wins this round, but it isn't the end by a damn sight. I'll get him in the long run, if it's the last thing I do."

He rather enjoyed letting his mind dwell on that. Once he was safe, his identity hidden under some other suitable cloak—he skipped over the difficulty of devising that—there would be time enough to consider the question of revenge on Grogan. It would give him something to live for; an incentive to get back to work and pile up a stake again. And there wouldn't be any hurry. Grogan would always be there, waiting. It was good to picture the terror Grogan would be feeling because of Henderson alive and plotting his downfall.

Although he couldn't stretch it out too long. Grogan would be busy, too. He would be digging away, with all his cop's tenacity, bulwarked by the law and all that money his wife had left him. Attending to Grogan would be both a pleasure and a necessity.

Henderson glanced at his watch and saw with surprise that the morning was gone. He looked toward the girl, who had not moved and who refused to return his gaze.

"What about knocking something together for lunch?" he asked.

"Lunch?" She sounded hypnotized.

"Yes, lunch. We've got to keep up our strength."

She rubbed a trembling hand across her forehead. "Marc, you must be crazy. How can you even think of food? Are we just going to sit here waiting for them to find out the truth about those ridiculous stories?"

"Of course not." Henderson restrained an impulse to laugh. She was so completely ignorant of his thought processes. "We take the night plane out of town. Until then, we have to sit here to throw sand in their eyes if they come back. Don't worry, they won't be certain about us until tomorrow at the earliest."

"But they won't let us get on a plane. You heard that policeman, and you saw how he looked. We wouldn't have a chance to get away."

Henderson patted his bald head. "You're forgetting the wig," he said. "And the skin stain and the rest of it. The flatfeet will be on the prowl for me and my daughter. Marcus Henderson won't even cross their minds."

She touched her own hair. It was a quick gesture, one she immediately tried to hide. Henderson saw that she was watching him with even more fear than before. Perhaps she was beginning to understand.

He didn't trouble to make it convincing. She might have her suspicions, but they wouldn't do her any good. She had no other out. She would have to trust him, and hope for the best. As long as she did not become completely hysterical, he was all right.

"What about that lunch?" he asked.

"I couldn't, Marc. I just couldn't. If you want to eat, you'll have to fix it yourself."

The lunch wasn't worth arguing about. Henderson wasn't hungry either, but he felt the need of some such gesture to prove the calmness of his nerve. He was, on the whole, pleased with the way he was taking this. Every conceivable step of this operation had gone wrong, through no fault of his own, and he was still in control where a lesser man would have cracked wide open. He would eat his lunch as though nothing had happened.

"All right," he said. "I'll be the cook. Maybe you'll have cup of coffee with me."

Both of them had been watching the pathway in front all morning, since Grogan and Mallory left. Surreptitiously, unwilling to let the other see, they had both been snatching glances at that strip of yard visible through the front window. Henderson looked again, before turning his attention to the food. The pathway was empty, of course. There had never been anything to see except an occasional passerby. Of course you couldn't tell which of the casual tourists was the man assigned to watch this cabin.

Satisfied that nothing had changed, Henderson opened the cupboard door and found coffee and bread. He didn't look for anything else—that would be enough to prove his point. There was nothing else but eggs, anyway, and the idea of an egg was not attractive. He turned on the faucet to fill the coffee pot.

A sound behind him sent him whirling around. The damned slut had the telephone in her hand. As he started toward her, she shrank back in her chair, clutching the telephone.

"Steve?" she said into the mouthpiece. "Steve? Steve?" Her voice was a mounting siren of terror.

Henderson struck the receiver from her grasp, while his other hand clutched furiously at her throat.

CHAPTER 17

Grogan and Mallory parted shortly after leaving the Green Grotto Motel. Grogan had been morose and silent while they walked back to the car, standing aloof while Mallory gave low-voiced instructions to his man stationed there.

"Well, Steve?" Mallory had said, when they were

seated in the police car again.

"It wasn't her," Grogan said. "Not Terry."

"Was it the other, then? Mrs. Carrol? You weren't so sure of that, before."

"Hell, I'm not sure now. Maybe there is some other explanation, and we are on the wrong track with both of them."

"Do you really believe that?"

Grogan did not know what he believed. His personal feelings were too deeply involved in this for his judgment to be secure. On the one hand was his almost hysterical desire for Betsy's safety. It led him to looking into shadows and perhaps seeing dangers not really there. Beyond that was his feeling for Terry, which he was only just beginning to realize. He had betrayed her, and nothing would ever be the same between them. Yet because of Betsy . . . Grogan was sorry, but he would have acted the same way again.

"I don't know," he told Mallory. "Drop me at the Carillon, Bill. I don't want to go to the hotel yet."

Mallory had protested, until assured by Grogan that he could see him to the door and that Grogan would wait there until Mallory returned later in the day or sent an escort for him. Grogan had no clear concept of why he wanted to go back to the Carillon. He only knew that he wanted to think, by himself, for a few uninterrupted hours.

And now he sat in the empty cabana, which seemed unnaturally quiet because of Betsy's absence. He had never been in the place in the daytime without her shrill chatter filling the rooms as she played. He had telephoned the hotel immediately on entering the room, and Vic had reassured him that all was well.

He had to face the problems of the future. Leaving

Henderson out of it, assuming for the moment that Henderson would be taken care of, Betsy had to be provided for. Not as they had been drifting along before the upheaval. Vic had made him see that, and now she and Rocco were taking themselves out of the picture. So there must be other arrangements.

Not a school. Remembering Lynn, he was very determined on that. A series of governesses, with no sense of security for Betsy, or one governess to whom she became too attached, was not the answer, either. He knew he must marry, in spite of the unpleasant memories of his own stepmother. It didn't have to be that way; he was not a weak-willed drunkard such as his father had been.

And yet you couldn't go out cold-bloodedly looking for a wife, considering only whether a woman was a suitable mother for your daughter. It wouldn't be the right sort of relationship; the type of girl he needed wouldn't be interested in him on that basis.

Which brought him back to Terry. She was, he saw now, the woman he wanted. One he loved enough to have married even with Betsy out of the picture, and yet who could give the little girl affection, the stability, the happy home life she needed. And now it was too late for that.

Memory of that scene in the grubby little cabin would always be between them. Memory of the time when Grogan had been so suspicious of her he had stood by while a policeman cross-examined her over a murder attempt. You couldn't build a future on that.

At one o'clock Grogan made himself a cup of coffee, which he drank while standing in the kitchen. He looked out the window toward the Bragg cabin; he could see no indication of movement. He found he didn't care one way or the other about that.

The telephone broke his reverie. He put down the cup and crossed the living room swiftly, scooping the receiver from the hook before the bell could ring again.

"Steve?" The voice was a breathless, terrified gasp. "Steve?"

Then the receiver roared in his ear as something crashed against the mouthpiece at the other end of the line. Grogan, suddenly taut with fear, could hear nothing more but an ominous silence.

He was running out the front door before he gave conscious thought to his course of action. Then, without breaking stride, he looked around for detective Harris, and could not see him. He continued toward the parking lot without hesitation. He could drive the two blocks to the Green Grotto in the time it would take him to set the police machinery in motion. She needed him, desperately, and right now. Grogan felt the chill certainty he would not be in time.

The Olds roared out of the parking lot, forcing an incoming tourist to brake to an emergency stop. Grogan wrenched the car around the corner and stamped the gas pedal to the floorboard. The big car answered with a neck-snapping surge. Within seconds he was jamming on the brakes and careening around the corner at the Green Grotto. His tires spurted dust and gravel on the roadway as he stopped in front of the Kelley cabin and leaped from the car.

The door of the cabin was shut; Grogan could hear no sound, and there was no one standing about. Without hesitation he lunged at the door, hitting it with his left shoulder with such force that the lock was torn from the jamb and he was catapulted into the room. His gun was in his hand as he stood looking about him.

The scene was astonishingly peaceful. Terry and Mike Kelley were seated at the plain kitchen table, staring at him with wide-eyed astonishment. Grogan breathed heavily, the intensity of his relief leaving him exhausted. He holstered the gun.

"You're safe," he told Terry, almost accusingly.

She left her chair and came to him, her arms gripping him as hungrily as he reached for her. Grogan held her for a moment of fierce ecstasy, all the rest of it forgotten.

"What's going on here?"

They turned to see the city detective assigned to the motel standing in the doorway. In his relief Grogan laughed aloud.

"Nothing," he said. "Nothing at all."

"Steve, of course I'm safe," Terry said. "What happened? Is everything all right?"

Grogan came back to earth: "I got a phone call," he said. "The girl just said: 'Steve.' She was in trouble. I was sure it was you, and I rushed over here."

"I didn't call. Believe me, Steve, I . . ."

Grogan laughed again. He felt wonderful, able to face her. "Believe you?" he said. "Of course I believe you. I rushed over here like a bat out of hell to save you from something or other. I wouldn't have done that if I had ever really had any doubts at all."

"Oh, Steve."

For the moment there was just the two of them, alone with their private realization. Only for a moment, until Grogan remembered with a stab of concern that he had after all not been imagining that frightened voice on the phone.

"Good God," he said, "it must have been Liza." And

to the detective: "We've got to highball to the Carillon. A woman calling for help there. We may be too late now."

Terry clung to his arm as he started toward the car. She was stronger than he would have imagined possible.

"No, Steve. It might be a trap."

"Even so, we've got to help her if we can." He held her shoulder with a brief, tight grip. "Call the station, honey. They'll send a car." To the detective: "Come on, Mack."

The city man had obviously been briefed on Grogan. He moved towards the Olds without hesitation. Still Terry clung to Grogan's arm.

"Think about Betsy," she said.

Grogan wavered. Then, to the detective, who was looking back impatiently over his shoulder: "You got any kids, Mack?"

"Sure. Two." The man clearly considered the question irrelevant.

Grogan looked at Terry. "You see? Call the station, and don't worry. Hurry, now."

Again the Olds roared out onto the highway. During the brief drive Grogan filled the detective in on events.

"It must have been happening right next door," he said, "and I missed it."

He felt sick at his own lack of perception. His first instinct had been to protect Terry, and his instinct was right in so far as it removed the cloud between them. But for Liza Carrol . . . Whatever he touched, Grogan thought, turned to blood.

They left the Olds in the middle of the Carillon lot and crossed the lawn at a run. Behind him Grogan could hear the thin wail of a siren.

They met Harris on the path. His worried frown dissolved at the sight of Grogan.

"Where the hell you been?" he asked. "I saw you light out and couldn't catch you. I've called the chief."

"I think there's trouble next door," Grogan said. "The girl phoned, and I thought it was someone else. Did you hear anything?"

Grogan was talking without breaking stride. Harris, running beside him, grunted a denial. Then he grasped Grogan's arm and dragged him to a stop several doors from the front of John Bragg's cabana.

"No sense to rushing it," he said. "It's quiet in there now. Either the girl is all right or we're too late to help her."

With neither Betsy nor Terry involved, Grogan was able to think clearly enough to see the sense in that. He studied the cabana, quiet and apparently deserted in the blazing sunshine. People scattered around the lawn watched them curiously. Mallory came toward them from the parking lot, running clumsily.

Grogan told the story briefly. Mallory grunted, frowning at Harris.

"How about it?" he asked. "Are they still in there?"

"How the hell do I know? They could have taken a powder when I went to call you, after I saw Grogan tear out."

"Yeah." Mallory turned toward the crowd beginning to gather around them. "You people stand back; there might be shooting here."

The bystanders moved away hastily. Mallory raised his voice.

"You in the house," he called. "John Bragg. Are you in there?"

The detective from the Green Grotto, on a motion

from Mallory, had moved to the rear of the row of cabanas. Harris worked his way along the intervening cabins, keeping out of the possible line of fire, until he stood at the corner of the house beside the front window. Grogan and Mallory remained where they were. No answer came from the cabana.

"Well," Mallory said, "I guess we go see."

"I'll take it," Grogan said.

"No." Mallory's voice was tough. "This is still my town, damn it!"

Grogan let him move ahead, because Mallory wanted it that way. He watched the big man move cautiously along the route Harris had taken, watched him pass the detective and step quickly to the porch and pause at one side of the door, pressing back against the wall. Only then did Mallory draw his gun.

"Bragg," Mallory called. "It's your last chance."

Only silence from within. Mallory lifted a foot and crashed it against the door; it swung inward. Mallory followed with a diving rush.

Grogan covered the distance quickly, but he was behind Harris when they went in the doorway. Mallory was standing in the middle of the room, his gun pointed at the floor. The place was empty, except for the body of Liza Carrol on the floor beside the telephone.

CHAPTER 18

Henderson had struck the phone from Liza's grasp, while his other hand closed around her throat and twisted it in a spasm of anger. He heard the bone snap; the gasping, gurgling cry was not needed to tell him he had finished her. Henderson scarcely gave the matter a thought as he dashed to the window and peered anxiously outside.

He saw Grogan running across the lawn away from rather than toward him. Another man came out of a cabana several doors to the north, and followed Grogan. The second man, though running, was traveling more slowly.

Henderson turned toward the bedroom, moving with clumsy haste. He had somehow been given unexpected time; perhaps only minutes, but he would have to make it do. He stumbled over Liza's outstretched legs, and paused long enough for a bitter satisfaction at her death. The slut had tried to do him in with her last breath. Inexplicably, she appeared to have failed.

He opened a bureau drawer and took out the hairpiece, forcing himself to fix it into position with careful fingers. It would not do to hurry that too much. He pulled off his dark-rimmed glasses and squeezed the contact lenses into place. The discarded pair he tucked into his coat—no sense leaving them around for the police to find and wonder about. The tube of complexion lotion also went into his pocket; that was a time-consuming operation, for which he did not dare to wait.

He hesitated a moment over whether to leave by the door or one of the bedroom windows. He decided on the door. The man who followed Grogan was probably the police guard, and he would attract less attention from the casual passerby if he simply walked out the door. He took a deep breath and stepped out into the open, his muscles tight with fear and his hand clutched around the butt of the .32 automatic in his pocket. No one paid him any attention as, without haste, he cut across the back portion of the Carillon's grounds and walked to the highway.

So far, so good. The highway was lined with service stations and motels. Henderson strolled toward the nearest station, where both attendants were busy at the gas pumps. He stepped unnoticed into the men's room at the back.

Locking the door behind him, Henderson hastily set to work on his face and hands with the lotion. The operation could not be hurried; it had to go on just so, without streaking or blotching. Twice he heard the door rattle as some impatient motorist tried the latch. Henderson kept at it until he was satisfied. The tautness of the muscles relaxed as the mirror gave him back the reflection of the dark-faced man with the brown, wavy hair who looked so unlike the John Bragg of earlier in the day.

As he stepped out the door he heard a siren, coming from the direction of the city and coming fast. The fear returned, overwhelmingly, and Henderson stood shaking as the car slowed down almost in front of the station and turned into the entrance of the Casa Carillon. Providentially, a bus had halted at the corner a few feet away, waiting for the siren to pass. Henderson made himself walk to it and tap on the doorway; he could hardly believe his good fortune when the door opened and the driver greeted him with a cheerful grin.

The next few hours were a torment to Henderson. He did not dare check into a hotel, and he knew a bus station or the airport would be the most dangerous place possible for him. Walking the streets was senseless, as it exposed him to just that many more prying eyes. He felt like a man in the spotlight, with a crowd following his every move.

And he was alone. For the first time, he was completely, entirely, alone. Always before there had been Charley Norris or some of the boys. Or a woman. Lately, Liza. Henderson could not restrain his sorrow for himself that she had made him kill her and so left him alone.

That was ridiculous, of course. He had to be alone, he was better off this way. Now there was no one to give him away, or to share his secrets. This was the way he wanted it. He bought a ticket to a movie and sat gratefully in the darkened house for the rest of the afternoon, oblivious of the pictures on the screen. He felt safely anonymous there in the dark.

An hour before plane time he left the theater and stepped out into the bright light again. It hurt his eyes, made him shrink back for a moment into the foyer, before he asserted his courage and stepped boldly to the curb, hailing a passing cab. There was nothing to be afraid of. Just this one last gamble, and he would have it made. He directed the driver to take him to the airport.

Henderson felt pleasantly exhilarated as he approached the desk. It was a bustling place, and no attention was being given to him. He told himself he was ahead of them in this, as he had always been ahead. Only the caution of habit made him pause and survey the group before the desk.

Two women, a small boy, and a man about his own size and age, a man with curly brown hair, wearing a light tan suit. Nothing at all remarkable about him— an ordinary businessman waiting while the women arranged for their tickets. And then he saw the two burly strangers close in on the man, one on either side.

One of the newcomers touched Tan-suit on the arm; the other stopped a few feet away, his hand in his pocket, a picture of wary watchfulness. He was careful not to let his partner come between him and Tan-suit. Henderson turned hastily to the magazine counter and pretended to examine the rack of paperback novels while he took in the scene. He saw the two detectives march the protesting traveler out of the building, and he fully understood the meaning of what he saw. The place was crawling with cops on the lookout for Henderson. The old Henderson, with the curly hair and the dark skin. Henderson as he stood there that moment. But they had not seen him yet.

The shaking, tearing fear was back on him as he walked stiffly to the men's room on the far side of the building. With every step he expected to feel a touch on his arm, but he made it. Their attention must be concentrated on the ticket desk. He went directly into one of the lavatories and locked the door behind him. He stood there for a long time, trembling, more hopeless than he had ever been in his life.

That damned Grogan. Somehow he had figured it out, tied John Bragg and Henderson together, and now the dragnet was out for both men. For him. Always it was that damned Grogan.

The thought brought restoring anger to Henderson. So he was finished. He would never get out of this stinking little town in the middle of the desert. He found he could accept that, as long as he still had something to work toward. Grogan. That was the only target to make the finish of Henderson worthwhile. He was going to take Grogan with him.

His hands were steady again as he pulled the tube of skin lotion from his pocket. He could still finish Grogan. All Grogan cared about was his kid, she was the blue chip in the game to him. Well, Henderson could fix that. As long as he had to go himself, he would get some satisfaction from making Grogan lose that most important possession.

He took off the hairpiece and stuffed it in his pocket. Using a hand mirror from his billfold, he went to work on the gleaming bald head, turning it the color of the rest of his skin. He had to work slowly; because the mirror was awkward, but he was in no hurry. He didn't mind postponing that walk back through the lobby.

Satisfied at length, he studied his reflection in the small mirror. Not too bad. Not good enough to risk close scrutiny at the desk, but it might get him by on the street. After consideration, he removed the contact lenses and assayed a slight squint in his left eye. It would have to do.

Henderson made it through the lobby and out to the cabstand without being accosted. He stepped directly into a waiting cab and had himself driven back to the center of town. There he paid off the driver, proud that he could do it casually and without a show of fear. Hell, he didn't feel fear. His mind was made up; this was worth checking out for. He began to look forward to the meeting with a pleased excitement.

He went into a drugstore and dialed police headquarters from the public phone booth at the rear of the store. He told the answering voice be wanted to speak to the chief.

"What's on your mind?" the policeman asked. "The chief is busy. Maybe somebody else can help you."

"It has to be the chief," Henderson insisted. "Or his

pal Lieutenant Grogan. You'd better put me through. They would want it that way."

"Just a minute." The heavy voice quickened with interest. "Hold on there. I'll see about the chief." And after a long silence: "The chief ain't here right now. I'll put you through to the chief of detectives."

Henderson had counted on that. He grinned to himself, almost gleefully.

"I don't talk to anybody else. It has to be the chief or Grogan. Tell me where I can reach Grogan. If I can get him in five minutes I can put the arm on John Bragg for him."

Another silence, no doubt with a hand muffling the mouthpiece, while they considered.

"I'm hanging up," Henderson said.

"Just a minute. Hold on. All right, you can call Grogan at the Crown Hotel."

Henderson left the drugstore and walked down the sidewalk to the first bar; he went in there, feeling none of the fear and hesitation which had pursued him since he left the cabana. He had become fatalistic. He had tried everything he knew, and luck had been against him. As far as his personal survival was concerned, the game was finished. He wasn't going to get out of town alive, unless he chose to go in handcuffs.

He ordered scotch, looking the bartender boldly in the eye as he did so. The hell with them. Nobody was going to recognize him until he had a chance to even the score with Grogan. He tossed the drink down, and another. He felt relaxed, powerful. No handcuffs for him. They would be scurrying around after him in every rat hole in town, and he was going to walk in the front door of the Crown Hotel. The last place they would expect him. He wasn't going to win, but Grogan was sure as hell going to lose.

Henderson took another cab to the hotel. He got out in front of the marquee, deliberately lingering over paying the driver. He nodded to the uniformed patrolman standing near the swinging door of the hotel; he was amused by the respectful response. Henderson felt ten feet tall. Not conspicuous, as he had before, but powerful, capable of anything. Even the searing anger at Grogan took a back seat to his calm confidence. He wouldn't let the anger trick him into a false move again.

He crossed the sparsely occupied lobby without hesitation. A bellboy, carrying two bags, was following a guest into the elevator. Henderson stepped in after them. He heard the bellboy tell the operator to stop at five, so Henderson said: "Four, please." A man idling beside the elevator had moved closer to the door when Henderson entered; on hearing the floor requested, he stepped back again. Although he was not nervous, Henderson acknowledged relief that he had not accidentally chosen Grogan's floor.

He got out of the elevator at the fourth floor. Moving without haste, he walked down the hallway to the stairs and followed them to the floor above. He was standing beside the elevator in the empty hall when the bellboy came around a corner, alone.

Henderson lifted the gun from his pocket long enough for the boy to see it, then returned it to the pocket, where he kept the muzzle pointed through the fabric. He was amused at the youngster's suddenly pasty complexion.

"Take me into an empty room," Henderson said. "Quick."

"I . . . I can't. They're all locked."

"Better figure a way. There never was a bellhop who couldn't get into an empty room."

Henderson didn't try to keep the old, familiar fury at being thwarted from roughening his voice. The time for that was past. He could enjoy the luxury of doing exactly as he pleased in this last crashing climax. The boy blinked and turned hastily toward a door opposite the elevator. He took a key from his pocket, fumbled with the lock for a moment, and the door opened.

Henderson pushed him inside the room and shut the door behind them. He took out the gun and pointed it.

"You're doing better," he said. "You just might live through this. Tell me what rooms the cop and his family are hiding in."

CHAPTER 19

Grogan knelt beside the body of Liza Carrol, feeling for a pulse he knew was not there. He got clumsily to his feet, ignoring the bustle in the cabana as the officers searched hastily through the other empty rooms. Grogan stood alone by the window, having his moments of regret.

She had been no good, of course. She was tied in with the attempts on his life, and with the threats against Betsy. Still, she could not have been with those others all the way. She had turned to Grogan at the end, with a call for help he would be a long time forgetting, and Grogan had guessed it wrong. He couldn't bring himself to look again at the body on the floor. He tried to find consolation in the thought that death from the broken neck must have been instantaneous. He would have been too late even if he had recognized her voice.

Mallory was talking into the phone, his voice insistent. He was giving headquarters a detailed description of John Bragg, arranging for a dragnet. He hung up the receiver and turned to Grogan.

"We'll get him," he said. "It's a small town. And no way out that we can't tie a net on. We'll get him."

Grogan heard a commotion at the door, where a detective was blocking the passage. Terry was calling: "Steve, Steve," her voice strained and frightened. Grogan shouldered his way past the man at the door.

"I'm all right," he told her.

Terry was a small, white-faced figure on the porch. Mike Kelley stood beside her; the rest of the gathering crowd remained on the graveled path and the lawn. She looked searchingly at Grogan.

"Really, Steve?" she asked. "Are you really?"

Grogan took her hand and smiled at her. He recognized some of the protective tenderness he felt toward Betsy. This was it; this was right. He became aware of Mike Kelley tapping his shoulder.

"Maybe we should meet again and start all over," Kelley said. "I wasn't at my best when you dropped in this morning."

Terry said: "Oh, Dad," exasperation mingled with the affection in her tone. She stepped back from Grogan.

Grogan shook hands with Mike Kelley, amazed at the transformation in his appearance during the last few hours. He had not really noticed him when he had gone rushing to Terry after the phone call. Now Kelley was natty in a linen suit, his carefully combed dark hair taking years from his age. Grogan blinked as he remembered how Kelley's bald dome had gleamed as he lay against the pillows.

"What's with the hair?" Grogan asked.

Kelley smirked. "An excusable frivolity, I think. It expresses my personality better."

Grogan stared at him. God, he had been blind. Inexcusably stupid.

"Mallory," Grogan shouted.

Mallory came to the door. "What's up?" he asked.

"Take a look at Kelley," Grogan said. "The hair."

Mallory gave Kelley a casual glance. He frowned, annoyed that Grogan should be wasting his time with trifles. Grogan seized his arm and pulled him out onto the porch.

"The hair," Grogan said again. "Remember how he looked before? Now think about John Bragg. Think how he would look with a top piece like that, only brown and a little curly. Think about him with his skin darker than it was today. You know what you've got?"

Mallory only looked wonderingly at him.

"You've got Henderson," Grogan said. "Marcus Henderson. Right under my nose for days. Go put that on your dragnet."

Grogan and Terry rode to the hotel together in Grogan's car, with a police cruiser pacing them for protection. Grogan knew he should have been filled with exultation at the prospect of running Henderson to earth. Here, knowing what they were looking for, they could hardly lose him. He found that he didn't care too much. He would be glad when it was over, of course, but the driving anxiety was gone. Henderson was finished. He was sure of that. The deep animosity and fear which had made him want a personal hand in that finish were gone. He was willing to leave it to Mallory.

"We . . . we have lots of things to talk about," Terry said hesitantly.

Grogan's hand left the wheel to cover hers.

"No, we don't," he said. "It's all settled. You must realize that."

"He is my father," she said. Almost defiantly. "I could never . . ."

"So he's your father. And if you mean he will always be your responsibility, that's all right by me. If he wants to live with us, fine. If he wants to wander off, we'll keep a candle in the window. Betsy is my kid, too. She'll be underfoot all the time." Grogan shot her a quick look, more concerned than his light tone admitted. "Will you find that hard to take?"

Terry clutched his fingers. "Oh, Steve, no. Steve, I'll do the very best . . ."

Grogan was filled with a deep content. Something he never expected to feel while Henderson was still on the loose. This was a happiness he had thought he would never experience again.

Betsy met them in the hotel, miraculously choosing this moment to be effusively friendly to Terry. She grasped Terry's hand and smiled up at her.

While Betsy led Terry to her room to be read a story, Grogan filled Vic and Rocco in on the events of the day. Vic blinked back unaccustomed tears.

"Oh, Steve," she said. "About Liza . . . how horrible. How could I have been so wrong.... She seemed to me to be so good with Betsy, so really fond of her."

Grogan said: "Maybe she was. She turned to me at

the end, remember. For all the good it did her."

"Forget the hearts and flowers," Rocco said, scowling. "We aren't out of the woods yet. Not while that joker is running around loose. "I'd still feel better if we were taking a hand in it. You're the only one who can spot this Henderson for sure."

"No." Grogan was positive. "I've been all wrong on this, Rocco. Look at the men dead already. And the girl—that's the hardest for me to face. They're dead because I turned outside the law."

"They had it coming. They would have gotten it sooner or later anyway."

The afternoon wore along. Grogan watched Betsy playing with Terry. He also watched Vic, and with more concern. This was going to be tough on Vic, following the course she had laid out for herself. He owed a lot to Vic. She seemed composed and even happy, buoyed up by an inner content. Only Rocco prowled the room nervously.

"Relax," Grogan told him. "We've got a cordon of cops around the hotel. There's a cop right outside the door. And we'll get a call pretty soon telling us Henderson has been caught. Take it easy."

The phone rang then. Grogan picked up the receiver to hear Mallory's voice.

"Has anyone tried to get in touch with you, Steve?" Mallory asked.

"No. Why?"

"Somebody called the station and said he had a hot tip he would give only you or me. The boys told him you were at the hotel."

"No contact here."

"Oh, well. Just a nut, I suppose. I'll call you when I hear anything."

Grogan frowned at the dead phone. That anonymous call to the station bothered him—he wondered if he had this figured right, after all. He had been convinced that Henderson was alone and on the run. Now it sounded as if he were known to at least one other person in town. And if Grogan had been wrong in thinking Henderson was alone, he might be missing the boat elsewhere as well.

Rocco started to ask a question, but he had got no further than "Was that—" when he was interrupted by a rap on the door.

Rocco crossed to the door, his hand on his hip pocket. "Yeah?" he said.

"Bellboy. Telegram for Mr. Grogan."

Grogan watched Rocco open the door. It was all right, or the patrolman on duty in the hall would have taken a hand. He gave the interruption only half of his attention; he was still thinking about the call from Mallory. He did not come fully alive until the figure in the hotel uniform had brushed past Rocco and stood menacing the room with a gun.

"Henderson!"

"That's right. You see where this is pointing, don't you, Grogan?"

They all saw. It held Rocco frozen against the wall, his hand still behind him, and it held Grogan motionless in his chair. The gun was pointing straight at Betsy.

Henderson, watching Rocco from the corner of his eye, spoke tersely. "Get over there by Grogan, where I can see you good. And keep your hands in sight. One move and I shoot the kid."

Rocco complied with slow reluctance. Grogan, studying Henderson's expression, felt a twist to the searing fear already gripping him. This wasn't a man come to make a deal; a man to whom he could talk sense. One look at those staring, triumphant eyes and the jumping pulse in the tense throat muscles told him that Henderson was past the point of self-control. He was here only for revenge.

"Daddy!"

Betsy, frightened, started toward Grogan. Terry held her back, struggling for a moment, until Henderson crossed to them with a quick step. He struck Terry to the floor with one backhand blow. With the same hand he grasped Betsy. And Grogan could only sit without moving, because through it all the muzzle of the gun had never wavered from Betsy.

"Just stand there a minute, honey," Grogan said. "There is nothing to be afraid of. The man is playing with you."

Betsy began to cry. She cried quietly, making no effort to get away, and her eyes watched Grogan reproachfully. Only the gun, held almost at the back of her head, kept him from moving.

"How do you like it, lieutenant?" Henderson asked. "What will this get you?"

"What I want most in all the world," he said. "This will even the score, Grogan. Tell me, what could I do that would make you suffer more than anything else?"

Grogan knew complete despair. In this frame of mind, Henderson was interested only in harming Betsy. He knew too well that he could destroy Grogan that way. Grogan, his brain numb, was still able to curse his own slow comprehension. He should have made his try while Henderson was crossing the room. It would have been a better gamble than this was going to be.

Grogan still carried the .38 in its belt holster. He was quick with it. Had the other weapon been menacing him, he would have taken a chance, secure in the knowledge that even if Henderson got him Rocco's shot would have blended with the others. But the gun was not pointed at him.

"Think about it, Grogan," Henderson said. "Just a minute. And if you believe I'm kidding, you should see what happened to the kid who was wearing this uniform and the cop out in the hall."

Grogan set himself to pull his gun. It would be awkward, from a sitting position, but it was the only hope. Self-preservation is a strong instinct; there was the slight chance that in the face of another gun Henderson would forget his resolution and try to get Grogan first. That was all Grogan could hope for.

There was a stir of movement beside him as Rocco stepped away, to stand beside a small end table near an easy chair. When Rocco spoke he sounded frightened.

"Don't you guys start shooting in here," Rocco said. "Hell, what does it gain you?"

The interruption had no effect on Henderson. In the same taunting tone he said: "One more step and I pull this trigger, copper. Don't play games with me. Tell him not to move again, lieutenant." Then he laughed, a high, breaking sound. "But it don't make much difference, does it? It's going to happen in a minute anyhow."

Grogan saw what Rocco had in mind. The move had pulled him sufficiently to one side so that Betsy and Henderson stood in line in front of him, whereas Henderson was behind Betsy from Grogan's point of view, his gun hand hidden. Rocco had the better target, and with Henderson's attention fixed on Grogan he would have a split second's better chance.

Grogan knew he had to leave it to Rocco, and it was the bitterest decision he had ever made. He would have to stand on the sidelines watching, while the biggest gamble of his life was being played by someone else. All he could do was hold Henderson's interest for another moment.

"We can still deal," Grogan said. "I'll promise to get you out of town. How about it?"

He saw Rocco's hand close around a small glass ash tray standing on the end table. He saw that without ever seeming to take his eyes from Henderson's, and then he didn't look again. He dared do nothing to distract Henderson. He even felt a small surge of hope. The tray would be quicker than a gun, and it would have the same result if it hit the hand menacing Betsy. It would be better than a shot in the body, which might pull the trigger even as Henderson died.

And yet the target was so small. Rocco was a baseball player; he must be sure he could hit the hand. Grogan knew that was ridiculous. Rocco could only hope to hit it, because it was the best chance left to them. And Grogan had to let him do it because he could think of nothing more likely to succeed.

"How about it?" he asked again.

That minute was an eternity to Grogan. He saw Betsy watching him tearfully and failing to understand why he left her alone with the frightening man. He saw Terry, motionless where she had been struck down. Terry was not hurt—she was looking up at Betsy in an agony of terror for the child. Vic had not moved from her chair.

"You know better, lieutenant," Henderson said.

Grogan sensed, rather than saw, Rocco's movement. He saw the ashtray skim across the room, and dared not move himself so long as Henderson's eyes were fixed on him, noticing nothing else. He saw Henderson's right hand knocked to one side as the ashtray hit it, saw Terry grasp Betsy's ankles and pull her feet from under her, before he was free to cross the room in a diving rush.

He heard the gun explode in Henderson's hand and knew that Betsy was not in the line of fire, and then he had Henderson's wrist clamped in his own hand while he clubbed him to the floor with the other. Dizzy with relief, he heard Betsy wailing and the babble of Terry's and Vic's voices.

Rocco pulled him away from Henderson. Rocco's dark face was strained with passion, and he had his own gun in his hand.

"Get them in the other room, Steve," Rocco said. "I'll take care of this."

Grogan picked up Betsy and comforted her, feeling the unbearable pleasure of her wriggling, unharmed little body pressed against his. He put his other arm around Terry, pulling her into the family circle. He shook his head at Rocco.

"No," he said. "Not that way. Just make a phone call, and let them pick him up. We're going out of this with cleaner hands than we went in."

THE END

Louis King was born Oscar Lewis King on June 28, 1898 in Christiansburg, Virginia. He became a film director but started his career in 1919 as a character actor specializing in villains and bullies. Sometimes credited as Lewis King, he began directing westerns and adventures films during the  silent era. He had a flair for outdoors pictures, *Powder River* and *The Lion and the Horse* being two good examples. In the 1950s, King began directing westerns for TV including episodes of *Gunsmoke, Zane Grey Theater* and *The Adventures of Wild Bill Hickok*. *Cornered* is his only novel. King died as the result of injuries sustained from a car accident on September 7, 1962 in Los Angeles.

BLACK GAT BOOKS offers the best in reprint crime fiction from the 1950s-1970s. New titles appear every month, and each book is sized to 4.25" x 7", just like they used to be. Collect them all.

Harry Whittington • A Haven for the Damned #1 •

Charlie Stella • Eddie's World #2

Leigh Brackett • Stranger at Home #3

John Flagg • The Persian Cat #4

Malcolm Braly • Felony Tank #6

Vin Packer • The Girl on the Best Seller List #7

Orrie Hitt • She Got What She Wanted #8

Helen Nielsen • The Woman on the Roof #9

Lou Cameron • Angel's Flight #10

Gary Lovisi • The Affair of Lady Westcott's Lost Ruby / The Case of the Unseen Assassin #11

Arnold Hano • The Last Notch #12

Clifton Adams • Never Say No to a Killer #13

Ed Lacy • The Men From the Boys #14

Henry Kane • Frenzy of Evil #15

William Ard • You'll Get Yours #16

Bert & Dolores Hitchens • End of the Line #17

Noël Calef • Frantic #18

Ovid Demaris • The Hoods Take Over #19

Fredric Brown • Madball #20

Louis Malley • Stool Pigeon #21

Frank Kane • The Living End #22

Ferguson Findley • My Old Man's Badge #23

Paul Connolly • Tears are for Angels #24

E. P. Fenwick • Two Names for Death #25

Lorenz Heller • Dead Wrong #26

Robert Martin • Little Sister #27

Calvin Clements • Satan Takes the Helm #28

A Black Gat Book
32
TEARS FOR JESSIE HEWITT
A Black Gat Book
26
Dead Wrong
Larry Holde
A Black Gat Book
33
REPEAT PERFORMANCE
William O'Farrell
A Black Gat Book
21
STOOL PIGEON
Louis Malley
"Every page of Stool Pigeon feels real and true."
—Elgin Bleecker, The Dark Time
Black Gat Books

William H. Duhart • The Deadly Pay-Off #41
Robert Ames • Awake and Die #42
Charles Runyon • Object of Lust #43
Paul Conant - Dr. Gatskill's Blue Shoes #44
Asa Bordages - Murders in Silk #45
Darwin Teilhet - Take Me As I Am #46
Stephen Marlowe - Blonde Bait #47
Jonathan Latimer - The Fifth Grave #48
Andrew Coburn - Off Duty #49
Basil Heatter - Any Man's Girl #50
Day Keene - Acapulco G.P.O. #51
John P. Browner - Death of a Punk #52
Glenn Canary - The Trailer Park Girls #53
Jacquin Sanders - Freakshow #54
John & Ward Hawkins - The Floods of Fear #55
Richard Jessup - Night Boat to Paris #56
Arnold Drake - The Steel Noose #57
Bait - William Vance #58
Jay Flynn - Drink With the Dead #59
Charles Burgess - The Other Woman #60
Gil Brewer - Wild #61
Thomas B. Dewey - Hunter at Large #62
Martha Albrand - Remembered Anger #63
Conrad Dawn - Chartered Love #64
H. Vernor Dixon - Too Rich to Die #65
Lee Wells - Day of the Outlaw #66
Elliott Gilbert - Vice Trap #67
Emmett McDowell - Switcheroo #68

Stark House Press
1315 H Street, Eureka, CA 95501 (707) 498-3135
griffinskye3@sbcglobal.net www.StarkHousePress.com
Available from your local bookstore or direct from the publisher

www.ingramcontent.com/pod-product-compliance
Lightning Source LLC
Chambersburg PA
CBHW071323150726
47997CB00002B/587